Bronx

By
Avery Gale

PUBLISHER
Avery Gale™
averygale.com

Editors: Sandy Ebel, Personal Touch Editing, and Karen Bailey

The Adlers

The siblings. Their occupations and ages at the beginning of the series:

Austin – 31 – CEO of the family oil conglomerate based in Austin, TX. Married to magical, Charlotte.

Asia – 30 – Ruthless legal eagle for the family business. Married to Franklin Cordesi.

Bronx – 29 – Owns a string of car dealerships in partnership with brother, Cleveland.

Cleveland – 28 – Race car driver. Astral traveler. Married to Vienna Quan.

Brooklyn – 27 – Retrieval expert for big insurance companies. Semi-retired in subsequent books. Security consultant. Married to Luke Grayson, lives in New Mexico. Daughter, Crystal.

Catalina – 26 – Freelance intelligent agent working with the CIA, MI6, Mossad, and others. Travels the world as a successful jewelry designer.

Israel – 25 – Security expert and tracker. Married to shifter, Dr. Bristol Banks.

Kensington – 24 – Actor. Married to Denali West.

London – 23 – Chemist/Researcher. Married to shifters, Elijah & Evan Monroe. They live outside Boston and have twin sons.

Paris – 22 – Recent College Graduate. Mated with Sheriff Trinity Stone. School Administrator and teacher.

Watch this page for updates in subsequent books in this series.

Prologue

Lost in Decade-Old Memories

B RONX ADLER SET his phone back on the glass top of his desk and looked out the floor-to-ceiling windows of his office, wondering what his mother was up to. She had called him every day for the past week, asking him to lunch or coffee. Not once had she mentioned his dad, which was odd since the two of them were ordinarily joined at the hip.

As the third of ten children, Bronx understood his parents' struggle to divide their attention, and they'd done a remarkable job of making all their children feel important. Bronx and his mother had always been particularly close in part because he was the most interested in the stories she'd been so anxious to share. He'd loved the tales of magicians, shifters, and the countless ways they'd influenced history.

Brighten Adler walked through the front door of his car dealership, the moon-and-stars print of her flowing skirt teasing the tops of her knee-high leather boots, the heels adding several inches to her petite frame. Bronx and his brothers had teased her relentlessly about using heels to delay the inevitable, but she continued to wear them. Hell, he and his brothers had been pre-teens when they'd passed her in height.

Bronx always thought her name was perfect because she brightened every room she entered, but studying her expression, he noted something different about her today. Her usual calm countenance was gone, replaced by a tension reflected in her rigid posture. Her watchful gaze searching the room sent a skitter of warning up his spine. Getting to his feet, Bronx moved quickly out of his office to greet his mother when she stepped off the elevator.

"Mother, you look beautiful, as always. Would you like something to drink, or would you rather leave right away for lunch?" As well as he knew her, she could still surprise him with her unpredictability. Grasping his hands with her small, delicate ones, she pulled him down so she could kiss his cheek.

"Such a considerate son and easily ensnared once we stopped playing phone tag. It seems as though it was easier to connect with family and friends before cell phones. People were either at work, church, or a school function, easily tracked down if you were so inclined. Now that I think about it, perhaps it was easier because you didn't know who was calling. When the obnoxious contraption on the wall rang, you got up and answered it." She frowned and shook her head, sending a shimmer of light over the fall of her jet black hair.

Bronx couldn't hold back his smile. Brighten Adler was a gifted witch, a ferocious shifter when anyone she loved was in danger, and as easily side-tracked as anyone he knew.

"Do you have a minute to sit down and relax before

we leave for lunch?"

"I'm afraid lunch isn't going to work after all. Your father canceled his second round of golf and asked me to meet him at the Garden Room for lunch. Since he doesn't feel this meeting is necessary, I'd rather he not know I was here."

Bronx blinked in surprise. He knew his parents didn't always agree, but he'd never known them to keep secrets from each other.

"Don't look at me like I'm a criminal, sweetheart. It's just... well your father doesn't want to alarm me about the threat to our safety. He mistakenly believes what I don't know, won't hurt me—sweet, but inaccurate." Her shrug was too deliberate to be convincing. He'd never known his mother's premonitions to totally miss the mark. His inner alarms start to buzz. There had certainly been times when her suspicions were a tad skewed, but there was always an element of truth that was undeniable.

"If it's a safety issue, maybe we should call Israel to sit in on this conversation. After all, this is his area of expertise." Israel Adler was in the early stages of setting up his security business. So far, it wasn't paying the bills, but with his brother's exceptional instincts and relentless determination, success was a given.

"I didn't ask to see you because I'm worried. Fate never makes mistakes, and its course is rarely set aside for long." She gave a small wave of her hand, sending an arc of sparkling glitter into the air. It always amazed him how blasé she was about the less significant elements of her magic. They might have been easy for her to ignore, but he found them utterly remarkable. "Do you remember me telling you about my college friend, Lisa Star?"

"The one who gave you the amulet you wear?" Bronx could not remember his mother ever taking off the oddly designed necklace. He'd admired it once, and she'd told him it was a gift from a friend who'd entrusted her with one half of the powerful totem. She'd held it out from her skin for him to see, asking him to run a single finger over its surface. He'd been no older than twelve, but he still remembered the strange tingling he'd felt and how quickly the feeling of electrical power rushed through his entire body. His mother hadn't said anything, simply given him a knowing nod.

I knew it would be you. When the time is right, I'll pass it along to you. When you find the one holding the other half, you'll have found your mate—you will also know you're holding a powerful magical tool. When the pieces are close, those wearing them will have their magic amplified. Her long-ago words echoed through his mind as he saw her slide her hands beneath her hair.

"The time has come for me to pass this to you. Use it wisely and protect it with your life… that's what I'm doing now." With those strange words, she unclasped the chain, and before he could ask any questions, she'd placed it around his neck. Bright Adler's magical gifts were a light she never tried to hide, but this whispered incantation was one he'd never heard her use before. The chanted words made the charm warm against his skin before it vibrated softly for several seconds.

"Promise me you'll never let anyone take it from you and be patient as you wait for your mate—fate will never forget you." She'd brushed a stray lock of his black hair back into place and smiled. "Remember my words and know that I will always be with you. It may seem as though I'm gone, but I don't want you to ever forget... I'm only a heartbeat away." When he opened his mouth to speak, she shook her head, whispered, "I love you," then disappeared in a cloud of the whitest smoke he'd ever seen.

It was the last time he'd seen her. The next evening, he'd gotten the phone call that forever changed all their lives. Carrington and Brighten Adler died in a fiery car accident on their way home from a late dinner with friends. Falling to his knees, a wail of anguish wrenched from his chest, but no sooner had his cry of grief echoed through the room than the charm vibrated and warmed against his chest. Despite the crushing sadness, he'd managed to remember her promise. Her words were what got him through the first months of sorrow.

As one of the older siblings, Bronx understood how important it was to be strong for his younger brothers and sisters. He and his older brother shared the magic of a compelling voice. As businessmen, they both knew it was unethical to use their unique skill for monetary gain, but it didn't keep its use from creeping into their everyday lives.

When their parents died, Austin was immediately thrown into the deep end of the family business. Asia had been close to drowning in legal work related to an estate teetering on the brink of bankruptcy. So, looking out for the younger Adler siblings fell to Bronx. Everyone gave Austin credit for saving the business and eventually turning it into the multi-billion-dollar conglomerate it was now, but Bronx knew Asia's legal maneuvering had been a huge factor as well.

Over the past several years, the pain of losing his mom and dad was slowly being pushed back by the memories of all the fun and laughter they'd shared. Reminiscing the happier times initially made him feel guilty, but they eventually moved to the forefront. Bronx often marveled at the way they'd all thrown themselves into their careers. Paris had been busy settling into college life, and in many ways, her escape to the west coast had probably been a saving grace for the youngest but fiercely independent young woman. If she'd stayed in Austin, Paris would have been forced to live in Asia's shadow—it was terrifying to even consider how poorly that would have worked out. Their tenacity and focus on their individuals careers had served them all well, and as strange as it sounded, success was remarkably therapeutic.

Through the years, Bronx always kept his mother's words close to his heart—he'd even had them tattooed on his chest…

I'm only a heartbeat away.

Chapter One

B RONX ADLER PUSHED away from the cool brick wall facing the alley and shook his head in frustration. *Fucking hell.* Another wasted night. The air around him was practically cracking with a change he couldn't define. The storm predicted to roll in tomorrow morning was going to be early, but it wasn't solely responsible for how unsettled he felt. Bronx knew he'd be lucky to get home before the sky opened up. He hated being rained on in his human form, another contributing factor to his foul mood. Fucking hell, he was getting tired of trying to anticipate his little burglar's next move; it was damned humiliating being outplayed by a woman he'd never met. It was even more humbling to realize she was rapidly becoming an obsession.

Weeks of break-ins without a clear picture of her or a damned clue how she was getting in was pushing his patience past its limit. She was slipping around his newest security system as easily as she had the cheap one his sister, Brooklyn, scoffed about being child's play. A mountain of money later, state-of-the-art security systems were being installed at each dealership. He was bleeding fucking money, and so far, she'd waltzed past two of the new systems this week. Half the time, she was little more than a blur.

The whole situation was baffling. Why she was entering the offices when the only thing he'd ever known for certain she touched on his desk was a stapler. She'd slept on the sofas in his offices and used his private shower, but seemed meticulous about leaving things undisturbed. He knew she'd accessed their internet, skirting their system security to access several research sites. From what he could tell, she was finishing up an advanced degree in antiquities and mystical studies.

Brooklyn Adler spent years working as a retrieval expert for insurance companies around the world. B, as she was known to family and close friends, broke into public and private buildings to retrieve stolen artifacts, artworks, and jewels. To the utter amazement of her family, insurance companies around the world were more than willing to support her unconventional career, paying her more money than she'd be able to spend in a lifetime. Bronx doubted his little sister had touched any of the money generated by her share of Adler Oil.

When Brooklyn was in Texas for their brother Kensington's wedding, Bronx asked her to review his security and identify weaknesses. She'd managed to humble two of her brothers in one fell swoop. Israel Adler's security company designed several options for security systems when Bronx opened his first dealership—being the tight ass he was, Bronx went the cheapest route. His business had expanded so fast, Bronx was barely able to keep up with the exponential growth, and in the absence of any significant security concerns, he'd continued using a system so outdated, his sister had laughed in his face.

Each of his luxury model car dealerships was undergoing an extensive security review. The current protocols and systems were being updated, and she was still managing to waltz past security checkpoints without pause. Bronx spoke privately with each of his managers a few days ago, giving them vague excuses while emphasizing the importance of notifying him rather than the authorities if they encountered an intruder. Those chats hadn't been easy. He'd hired smart people, and they weren't easily fooled. It was easy to see the questions in their eyes—fortunately, they'd kept their inquiries to a minimum.

Bronx stood in the alley, hands-on-hips, and sighed in frustration. *Hell, at this point, I don't know if I'm pissed because I've invested a ton of fucking money on updating security for no apparent reason or because I'm being outplayed by a woman who has captured my attention before we've even met.*

KENYA STAR STOOD statue-still in the shadows. Barely breathing, her concentration began to falter, but she wasn't sure if it was because her damned brain was screaming for oxygen or the proximity of the man she'd been watching for months. The pendant that always laid between her breasts began vibrating as soon as she'd started walking down the alley. Had she been smart enough to back away? Hell no, she'd forged ahead as if she had every right to be there. If she wasn't well trained in silent movement, Bronx Adler would have heard her coming long before she would have known he was lying in wait.

Damn, she needed to step up her game or lose the opportunity to steal the other half of the magical totem she'd been looking for since her mother died. The gentle breeze blowing down the alley had been in her favor, but she felt the moment Mother Nature decided to play havoc with her good fortune. The man standing six feet in front of her pushed away from the brick wall, muttering to himself. For the first time, she envied a shifter's enhanced hearing.

Biting the inside of her mouth to keep from laughing, Kenya shook her head at the absurdity. Hell, at this point, she'd settle for normal hearing. A childhood infection damaged her eardrums so severely, she was rapidly losing the diminished hearing she'd dealt with since she was a teen. If the magic of the pendent was as powerful as she'd been told it would be after the halves were once again joined, Kenya's first spell would be to improve her hearing.

Great Goddess, what was she doing daydreaming? First, she had to finish her research and get her hands on the other half of the magical artifact. It was taking forever since she had to spend so much time covering her computer tracks, making it look as though she was working on some damned academic paper. *Like I have enough money to take classes.*

Kenya always dreamed of going to college, but her mother's nomadic lifestyle meant she'd never attended a traditional school. Without transcripts, she'd been forced to forge them, and money was always a problem. She'd been in Texas for months and only managed to take a couple of classes before winding up living on the street.

Once she'd started reading her mother's diaries and discovered her close friendship with Brighten Adler, Kenya had finally been able to point herself in a specific direction. She wasn't sure which of the Adlers had the magical pendant, but it only took one trip into Bronx's car dealership to know she was on the right track.

Lost in her memories, Kenya missed the first hint of a wind change. Lightning flashed, illuminating the rapidly cooling Texas night. The bright flash startled Kenya, breaking her concentration enough, she would definitely be visible to a shifter with enhanced night vision. Standing deep in the shadows wouldn't be enough to hide her from Bronx if he turned toward her. Damn it, she should have known better than to tempt fate by predicting the worst possible scenario. It was almost as if she'd wished this disaster into existence.

She saw his shoulders drop, wondering for half a heartbeat if the small tell was from resignation or if he was bracing for something she couldn't see. *Didn't take long to figure it cut, did it, Ms. Not Paying Enough Attention to what's happening. Pickle fudge.* The storm that had been predicted moved in early, shifting the slight breeze wafting through the alley to a full thunderstorm-worthy gale from the other direction between one heartbeat and the next.

Kenya watched as the world around her seemed to switch to slow motion. A deep growl came from Bronx's direction before he turned, his gaze zeroing in on her without any hesitation. Everything about the moment was electrified... his eyes glowing with a golden bronze light, Kenya was certain she would never forget. The pendant she wore vibrated so fast, she wondered if it would shatter the links of the chain. Watching as he pulled in a deep breath, his nostrils flared as he scented her, Kenya swore the lightning she'd seen in the night sky was now arching between the two of them.

"Mine."

The word was spoken too softly for her to hear, but his lips had been easy to read. The sky opened up, and rain began pounding down in torrents. Grabbing the heavy duffle at her feet, Kenya turned to run, shocked to discover her feet were no longer touching the ground. Holy hell, the man moved fast. One moment he'd been standing several feet in front of her, the next, he'd wrapped an arm around her waist, lifting her so gently, she hadn't felt the shift in her position until they were moving. When she tried to wiggle out of his hold, she felt his hold tighten.

"Oh no, you don't. I've been waiting my whole life for you." He practically snarled the words, making her wonder what he intended to do to her. *Hell, for all I know, he wants to eat me alive. I've read the damned books. Shifters love rare meat, but I thought it was the four-legged kind.* "Are you serious? You think I'd eat you?"

Pickle fudge, Kenya couldn't believe she'd said that out loud. He was practically running toward a car, and a shudder raced through her when his hand brushed over the bare skin between the top of her jeans and the hem of her cropped shirt. Heat flared deep in her core, and Kenya felt a level of desire she'd never experienced.

Shaking her head, she tried to push her body's reaction back and refocus her attention on the fact she was about to be stuffed into a car by a man she didn't know. Damn it, she needed to find the other half of the magical totem and figure out why hers was heating against her chest. The lights on a car parked a block away blinked a few seconds before he pulled the door open. Setting her on the soft leather seat, Kenya started to scramble back out before he could close the door.

"Stay where I put you, mate." His voice was rougher than it had been any of the other times she'd heard him speak. The man was something of a local television celebrity, his commercials always entertaining, and there was no question he was every woman's fantasy. Damn, he was gorgeous. Monkey butts, what was wrong with her? Why the hell was she still sitting in the car? Frack, she wasn't a child who could be ordered around. And what the holy heck did he mean when he called her *mate*?

He better be pretending to be Australian and not implying he plans to bite me. I should have read more about shifters and maybe researched in something more current than those scary old texts... and relied on a source more reliable than erotic romance novels she'd found in the musty used bookstores near campus.

Who was she kidding? She didn't have the money for more classes or books. It was hard enough to find a safe place to sleep at night. Breaking into Bronx Adler's businesses had been relatively easy, but now that he'd upgraded his security systems, it was riskier.

Bronx slid into the seat beside her and pulled a small towel from the backseat. "Here, let's get some of the water off you before I start the car. The air conditioning will turn you into a popsicle if we don't dry you at least a little."

Kenya sat in stunned silence as he patted the towel gently over her face and down both arms before running it roughly over his own face. A quaking shudder moved from her core to the surface, leaving a trail of heat in its path when he focused on her before turning the key to start the engine.

A rush of panic assailed her when she realized her duffle was gone—everything she owned was in the large bag. Frantic to find it, she reached for the door handle as the door locks engaged, and the ignition caught.

"Wait. My bag. It has everything I own." The moment the words slipped from her lips, Kenya knew she'd made a mistake.

"What do you mean everything you own is in the duffle bag?"

His large hand encircled her wrist, his touch setting of a new rush of heat, this one centering a lot lower than the first. Her entire body suddenly felt as though it was focused on her sex. The pendant and her pussy felt as if they were on parallel tracks of intense sexual heat. The more her mind focused on the need she felt building inside, the stronger the pendent vibrated.

"I'm sort of... well, I'm between places right now, so I'm... umm, traveling light." Great Goddess, she was going to get struck by lightning for sure. Lying was a big risk, but telling a big one during a thunderstorm seemed like an unnecessary challenge to fate. He studied her with an intensity Kenya thought was reserved for specimens under a microscope. Her gaze involuntarily dropped to where her hands were clutched in her lap. In her peripheral vision, she saw him shake his head. He was muttering under his breath, but she was only able to make a couple of words here and there.

"Your bag is in the trunk. You probably would have heard me close it if you hadn't been so lost in your thoughts." Checking his mirrors, Bronx pulled away from the curb and shook his head. "Just for the record, I've never pretended to be anything, and I wouldn't have the first damned clue how to fake being Australian." Kenya gasped, turning so fast in her seat, she almost slid off the slick leather seat. Pulling to the curb, Bronx leaned over her, pulling the seat belt into place. "Wear it—always. Your safety is now my number one concern."

"Why?" Kenya hadn't intended to ask the question aloud, but the heat she saw flare in his dark eyes made her glad she had. His fingers slid around the back of her neck before slipping into her wet hair. Tightening his hold, he tipped her head to the side and sealed his lips over hers. The kiss was as unexpected as it was hot. The pressure of his full lips against hers increased, ramping up her desire so quickly, Kenya felt her upper body lean forward, the unconscious need to be closer circumventing her self-preservation.

At first, she tasted the cool and refreshing hint of a late summer rain, but it was rapidly replaced by the urgency of a gusting wind moving across the wide-open prairie. She heard a soft moan and realized it was rumbling from deep in her chest. By the time he pulled back, Kenya couldn't remember why she'd been reaching for the door handle—heck, she'd be lucky to remember her own name after his bone-melting kiss.

By the time the fog in her mind cleared, they were once again driving down the street. It took her several more long seconds to pull herself together enough to ask where he was taking her. Panic started to settle over her, and she blurted out her concern in a rush of words.

"Are you having me arrested?"

His hands clenched on the steering wheel, and his jaw muscles tensed.

"Not hardly." Casting a quick glance in her direction, he asked, "What would I have you charged with? Since when is it illegal to stand in an alley?"

"Then, where are we going?" She shuddered in the rapidly cooling car and watched as he immediately reached for the air conditioning vents, repositioning them, so the cool air was directed away from her.

"We are both soaked to the bone. I want to make sure you are warm and comfortable before we chat." She'd spent a lot of time sleeping outside the past few months; being comfortable sounded like an unattainable luxury. "You said you are *between places* right now, so I figure that means your place isn't an option, so we'll go to mine."

Chapter Two

B RONX HAD BEEN shocked to the depths of his soul when the wind shifted in the alley, and her scent wrapped around him. He had no idea how long she'd been standing there, but since he hadn't heard a sound in all the time he'd been waiting, she must have been there when he arrived. Her sweet scent told him far more than she probably knew. His nose was particularly sensitive—every change in her emotions initiated a shift in her body chemistry.

When he'd first caught her, he'd sensed her hesitance, but there hadn't been any hint of panic or genuine fear. She had to know he was watching for her, studying her movements and habits—the security upgrades alone would have been a dead giveaway. Learning she was homeless explained why she was using the showers and probably the computer time as well. What he didn't know was where she'd been sleeping. Damn, the thought of his mate sleeping alone out on the street scared the hell out of him.

It would be more expedient to utilize one of the suites at Adler Oil, but taking her to his home felt right. It would also be more difficult for her to sneak away when the conversation became uncomfortable—and it would. Hell, one of the first questions he wanted to ask was why the damned pendant around his neck was vibrating. She remained quiet until he pulled onto the freeway.

"Wait. Where do you live? I don't want to be too far from... well, from town. What happens if I have to leave? It will be too far to walk back."

He had to give her credit—she was trying hard to cover her fear. It wasn't working, but she was certainly giving faux bravado a valiant try.

"Nothing is going to happen that will make you want to leave, I promise. If, for some reason, you feel like you have to return to the street in the pouring rain, I will help you make alternative arrangements." For the first time, he noticed the way she tilted her head whenever he spoke without looking directly at her. She was completely focused on his mouth—hell, she was reading his lips. Glancing at her ears, he caught the smallest glint of something resting on the top of her outer ear.

"What is your name?" Bronx deliberately whispered the word while looking to his left, and his suspicions were confirmed when she leaned closer and asked him to repeat what he'd said.

"I'm sorry I missed that. Could you repeat it, please?" It was clear to him she was dealing with a hearing impairment. He had several employees who dealt with similar challenges and understood some of the roadblocks it presented.

"I asked your name, *Cher*." He saw her eyes widen at the use of the endearment, a reaction he suspected she thought was hidden in the dimly lit car.

"Kenya Star. My name is Kenya Star."

It took him a few seconds, but he finally realized why the name sounded familiar. His mother had a friend in college with the same last name. Since he didn't believe in coincidences, he was going to wait until he could closely monitor her reactions before he asked if there was a connection.

"It's nice to meet you, Kenya. I assume you already know who I am, but in the interest of keeping my sweet mama from grabbing onto a bolt of lightning from her celestial home and smacking me with it for being rude, I'll introduce myself. I'm Bronx Adler, the owner of the businesses you've been breaking into the past several months." He saw the flare of panic in her eyes and shook his head.

"You have nothing to fear from me or my family, *Chef*. Hell, my sister, Brooklyn, is a fan. She spent years breaking into private and public buildings, retrieving stolen artifacts, and jewels for insurance companies. Once she learned you were able to skirt the new security measures, she made me promise to introduce you."

Exiting the freeway, Bronx turned toward the lake. Pressing the button to activate the gate, he saw her eyes widen when the car slipped through the heavy steel panels with less than an inch to spare on either side. He'd misjudged the opening a few times when he'd first moved in— those mistakes had been damned expensive, but he'd risen to the challenge. The learning curve had been steep but remarkably short, a fact his accountant appreciated.

"Wow. How many people live here? Is this one of

those packhouses I read about? Holy Humping Helen, is this a hotel?"

I drove around to the closest rear entrance activating the garage door, so we wouldn't have to walk through the rain to get inside—not that it was possible for either of us to get any wetter than we already were.

"This is not a packhouse. As a matter of fact, our pack has never lived together the way some do. I'm anxious to hear about your magical background, *Cher*. Your question suggests a certain level of knowledge about my kind, but first, I want to make certain you are safe." She would always be safe with him although he doubted she would believe him if he tried to reassure her. He didn't know why she was homeless, but it stood to reason she wasn't living on the street and breaking into his dealerships to shower because it was her life's dream—that didn't mean he wasn't skeptical about why she'd targeted his businesses.

Bronx suspected Kenya wouldn't willingly put herself in someone else's hands until they'd gained her trust. She'd relaxed marginally until he'd pulled onto the freeway, then sat ramrod straight until he promised they weren't going too far from downtown Austin. Her demeanor appeared calmer until they'd pulled into his garage. Turning to Kenya, Bronx placed his hand over the top of her forearm, stalling her when she would have reached for the door handle.

"No, *Cher*, wait for me to open your door. There will be times when it's a safety issue, and I want you to begin making it a habit to wait." Moving quickly to the passenger side of the car, Bronx opened the door and nodded his approval when she placed her small hand in his, allowing him to help her from the soft leather seat.

Bronx deliberately left her bag in the trunk—no need to make it easy for her to escape. Moving through the door leading to the mudroom, Bronx saw Kenya shiver when the cool air from the air conditioning moved over her.

"*Chef*, I want you to strip out of your wet clothes and leave them here." Reaching for the robe he knew was folded in a nearby closet, he frowned when he turned back to where he'd left Kenya, but she'd disappeared. "*Chef*?" If he hadn't been looking closely, he'd have missed the slight distortion of the framed picture hanging on the wall near the door.

"I've wondered a thousand times how you were able to hide from the cameras, but you were there all along, weren't you?" As she slowly reemerged from the camouflage, Bronx wondered what was more impressive, her magical skill or his first glimpse of her spectacular body. He was gobsmacked by how magnificent she was, despite what had to be the ugliest underwear he'd ever seen on a woman. She must have sensed his reaction because she started to fade once again. "Don't. You are fucking spectacular, Kenya." *And mine. You don't fully understand what that means yet, but it's still true.*

"Take off the rest, or this robe isn't going to do you any good." The deep red blush coloring her cheeks was a testament to her innocence. Chuckling silently, Bronx wondered when he'd last seen a woman blush. The utilitarian bra she wore slipped down her arms, revealing dusty rose nipples so tightly peaked, he knew they'd look spectacular in clamps When she finally slid the tattered white cotton panties down, his breath caught. The neatly trimmed patch of dark curls shielding her pussy did nothing to deter his desire. He appreciated her attention to grooming but couldn't wait to have her waxed smooth. Hell, just thinking about licking those pink folds sent a surge of blood to his cock. Wrapping her in the robe, he pulled her into his arms, marveling how perfectly she fit despite the considerable difference in their heights.

"Thank you for your trust, *Chef*. It means more than I can tell you." Taking her hand in his, Bronx lead Kenya to the master suite at the other end of the house. "Let me start the shower for you. It's tricky." Techy was probably a better term, but since she'd managed to bypass his best security system, he'd leave her to it if she wasn't shivering and turning an eerie shade of blue.

Shifters weren't intimidated by nudity, and he'd been pleased when she'd stripped without argument. He suspected her modesty would return if he gave her too much time to consider her situation. With the water running in the glass and marble enclosure, Bronx switched on the warming element of the towel rack. He doubted Kenya realized how rich in meaning her sigh had been as she'd looked longingly at the plush towels hanging over the rapidly heating rack.

"You won't need to worry about turning anything off, everything is in on timers." It would keep her from hiding out in the shower—a feature he'd happily override if they were showering together. Pushing his desire to the backburner, Bronx refocused his attention on his mate. Holding out his hand, he watched her eyes widen before her pupils dilated. He heard the hitch in her breath and smiled to himself as the sweet scent of her arousal assailed his senses.

"Give me the robe, Kenya. I'm going to make sure you get into the shower safely, then I'll lay out something for you to wear. When you're finished, I'll meet you in the kitchen." She slowly opened the robe, revealing... what the hell? How had he missed the pendant resting a few inches above her spectacular breasts? *Because you zeroed in on her nipples and let your fantasy about clamps blind you to anything else.* Reprimanding himself, he shook it off, deciding it was more important to get her into the shower than to begin asking questions.

The last thing he heard as he closed the door was her whispered, "Oh, I've died and gone to heaven." He smiled, knowing the pulsing shower was hot enough to warm the chilled surface of her skin and powerful enough to massage the tension from her tight muscles. Setting out one of his Oxford shirts before grabbing clothing for himself, Bronx headed down the hall.

Damn, it felt right having her here and knowing Kenya would be walking into the kitchen in a few minutes, wearing nothing but his shirt made him wish he could enjoy the benefits of her scanty clothing. He could hardly wait until they finished talking. It was going to be difficult to resist slipping his fingers between her slick folds. Waiting to find his mate seriously tested his patience, and he had a feeling waiting to claim her wasn't going to be any easier.

Chapter Three

KENYA WAS RELIEVED she hadn't stalled too long showering. She'd barely gotten the conditioner rinsed from her long hair when the water shut off. After Bronx left her alone, she'd quickly stepped back out of the enclosure to set her hearing aids on the counter. The small devices fit so far down in her ear canal, most people didn't realize she was wearing them. Goddess knows she didn't have enough money to replace them, so letting the small devices get wet wasn't an option.

Drying with a warm towel was pure ecstasy. Once she managed to get her own apartment, she was going to look for a warming rack. *What a joke. I'll be lucky to afford towels.* It seemed to take forever to comb the tangles from her hair. She usually kept the long locks in braids to avoid tangles and make it easier for her to tuck under a cap, but she'd been running late tonight and left the long strands to trail down her back. The second night she'd been forced to live on the street, Kenya discovered how vulnerable she was if someone grabbed one of the roped braids. She'd narrowly escaped and never forgot the lesson.

She shook her head when she saw a plain white shirt draped over the foot of the enormous bed. Looking around the large room while pulling on the shirt, Kenya was surprised the décor wasn't more masculine. Various shades of blue were accented by a soft rose and glittering silver. It was easy to see the room was designed as a place of relaxation. She wondered what lay behind the door in what she'd first thought was a bay window. The tray ceiling and crown moldings were stunning, the details accented by subtle lighting she suspected were designed to lend ambiance to the entire space.

Taking a deep breath, Kenya started down the hall. The wide plank flooring was cool beneath her bare feet, and she wished she had a pair of socks. Rounding the corner, Kenya gasped.

"Your kitchen is huge. How many people eat here? Do you cook for them, or do you have a caterer?" The questions tumbled out before she could pull them back, and she was relieved when she heard Bronx chuckle from where he stood in front of the stove. He was slowly stirring a pot, his eyes moving over her in a slow caress Kenya felt all the way to her core.

Bronx's low riding jeans were zipped, with the top button open, drawing her eyes to the dark trail of hair arrowing south. His feet were bare below the frayed hem of his jeans. There was something incredibly sexy about the way he was dressed, and she hoped he wouldn't notice her staring.

"You keep looking at me like that, *Cher*, and I'm going to set the soup aside for a few hours."

Hours? Holy cats!

"Sorry, you... well, you surprised me. I wasn't expecting you to be... umm, cooking... without... well, dressed like that." She gave a quick wave intended to take him in from head to toe, but her eyes paused when she noticed the sizeable bulge pressing relentlessly against the straining zipper of his jeans. Holy hailstones, the man was huge. Kenya had fantasized about him too many times to count, but now she wasn't convinced he'd even fit.

Just my rotten luck... a hot guy thinks I'm his mate, and I'm not experienced enough to give him what he'll want. I swear if my mother wasn't already dead, I'd do her in myself for getting me into this pickle.

They'd moved so many times when she was in primary school, truancy officials threatened to put her in protective custody. When a school official's complaints started to sound serious, her mother would pack them up in the middle of the night, and they'd be two hundred miles down the road by the time school started the next day. If her mother was simply tired of her current male companion, they'd flee during the day while he was at work. Her childhood had been filled with so much upheaval, Kenya often wondered what it would be like to know where you would be living a month from now. What it would be like to have a real Christmas tree and be confident Santa would know where to find you.

Blinking, Kenya pulled herself back to the moment and realized Bronx had moved so close, she could feel his body heat moving like a sensual breeze over her bare skin. He smelled so good, her body unconsciously leaned forward as she pulled in a deep breath.

"Fuck me, *Cher*, I was going to wait to kiss you, but everything about you is firebombing my good intentions."

He picked her up as though she weighed nothing and set her on the cool marble countertop. When she gasped, he moved in, taking advantage of the opening, his lips sealing over hers and his tongue moving against her own. Mint and a hot summer night—she'd never tasted anything or anyone else like it. His kiss was as sweet as it was demanding, and she wondered if any other man would light her up as quickly as this one had.

"Stop thinking and feel. Give yourself to me, *Chef*. Let me show you how perfect we are for each other." His lips pulled back from hers, pressing butterfly kisses along the edge of her jaw before moving to whisper in her ear, "Relax and put yourself in my care for the next ten minutes, then we'll eat and talk."

Feeling his body heating hers, Kenya tried to neutralize the way her body was responding but knew she'd lost the battle when his hand slipped between the front placket of the shirt to cup her bare breast. Her entire body heated with desire when he rolled her aching nipple between his fingers. Moaning, Kenya arched her back, pushing the tight nub deeper into his hand.

Walking down the hall, Kenya looked forward to finding out what smelled so delicious. Now, thoughts of food were the furthest thing from her mind. She'd read about people spontaneously combusting but always assumed it was a myth perpetuated by annoyed parents trying to control unruly children. She needed to rethink her assessment... later.

Bronx gave her nipple a firm pinch before pulling his hand from her shirt. The tight bud throbbed for several seconds before the heat was replaced by the sudden chill from the loss of his touch. It wasn't until her body stopped vibrating with need Kenya noticed the pendant was pulsing in time with her rapidly beating heart.

Lifting her from the counter, Bronx set Kenya on her feet, holding her until he knew she wasn't going to collapse into a heap.

"Let's eat before the soup is cold. I want to hear all about you, but first, I want to know you've had a good meal."

As she watched him ladle the thick soup into bowls, her stomach growled—loudly. She felt her cheeks heat with embarrassment, but his soft laughter made her feel better.

"Don't ever be embarrassed about being hungry, *Cher*. I have an appetite as big as Texas, and my siblings put me to shame."

BRONX KNEW HE'D lost Kenya when she sipped from the spoon and groaned happily. She mopped up the last of her soup with a thick slice of buttered sourdough bread and gave him a sheepish grin. Getting to his feet, he refilled her bowl, set it in front of her before nodding.

"When was the last time you ate a good meal, Kenya?" He knew from the way she refused to meet his gaze, he wasn't going to like the answer.

"I haven't really had enough money to eat full meals. Tuition costs doubled this year, so I am trying to save money to return to school someday. I'm cutting back everywhere I can."

Bronx was too stunned to respond for several long seconds. He wanted to reassure her money would no longer be an issue but knew it was too soon. The last thing she needed was to feel as though he was taking over her life. He didn't know much about her and could only imagine what she'd been forced to give up as she'd tried to make things work.

"I want you to promise you'll tell me when you're hungry, *Cher*. I'll never be too busy to feed you." He saw her eyes widen in surprise before they softened with a look of gratitude. Bronx knew he would never forget this moment or the sense of relief he felt move over him—an emotion he knew came from Kenya. Great Goddess, when was the last time a woman he'd taken out had given him even the smallest hint she appreciated the effort he'd put into a dinner date?

"I don't want to get spoiled. It will be too hard to go back to my life if I get used to all this luxury." He knew she'd tried to make it sound as though she was joking, but it was a wasted effort.

"Are you related to Lisa Star?" Bronx deliberately asked the question without any preamble, hoping her reaction would give her away if she tried to lie. He wasn't sure what he'd expected, but he felt like a first-class ass when her pale green eyes filled with tears. She set her spoon down without finishing her second bowl of soup, making him want to howl in frustration. Damn it all to hell, why hadn't he kept his mouth shut? Scooting his chair back, he pulled her to her feet and led her into the living room. When she tried to take a small chair as far from his lounger as possible, Bronx chuckled and shook his head.

"No, *Chef*, you'll sit with me. I want you close. It will help us bond during our conversation." She stiffened when he pulled her down on his lap, positioning her, so she was sitting sideways, her bare legs draped over the arm of the chair. Placing his hand atop her thigh, he almost laughed out loud at the way her eyes widened. He slowly caressed her upper leg with his thumb, brushing close enough to the sensitive crease at the top of her leg, the touch sent goosebumps racing over her soft skin.

"Talk to me, Kenya. Tell me why mentioning my mother's college friend brought tears to your eyes." He didn't force her to look at him, but he wouldn't usually allow her to hide by looking into the distance.

"Lisa Star was my mother. She died a few months ago." Her answer was spoken softly, but he appreciated the fact she'd been so direct.

"Did she know her friend died in a car accident?"

"I'm not sure. It was always hard to know what was real and what was her imagination. My mom was fun, but she was also the most irresponsible person I've ever known. I don't know if she was aware of your parents' deaths... I..."

Bronx knew when someone was holding back important information—he'd had plenty of experience dealing with siblings, employees, and customers. Drawing on a reserve of patience he hadn't known he had, he decided to use another tactic.

"Without moving, I want you to show me how you hide in plain sight." Almost immediately, he felt a surge of electricity warming her as the pendant against his chest rose off the surface of his skin. *What the hell?* He blinked, and she was gone—well, he could still feel her slight weight on his lap, but she'd disappeared from sight. "Amazing. You are going to drive me crazy just like Charlotte does, Austin." He chuckled when she faded back into view, her head cocked to the side in question.

"My sister-in-law, Charlotte, can shimmer out of sight. It's similar to what you just did, but she has trouble maintaining it for any length of time. She is also a healer. A word of caution—if she gets her hands on you, she's going to take on any pain or illness you're dealing with, then heal herself in record time. She will also know more about you than you might be ready to share, so consider yourself warned."

"That must be exhausting."

Bronx was impressed with Kenya's observation. There were so many people who would take advantage of Charlotte if they understood how powerful her gift was, but the entire Adler family made it their personal mission to shield her as much as they could.

"I'm not sure who suffers more, Charlotte or my oldest brother, Austin, because he is as protective as they come. The other issue with her magical ability is when Charlotte gets nervous, she shimmers into a mist." He couldn't hold back his chuckle. He'd seen his sweet sister-in-law dig herself into a hole more than once by disappearing when she thought her Dom was upset with her. "She also forgets how difficult the illusion is for her to maintain over an extended period." Fading back into view always seemed to coincide with the peak of Austin's frustration. *I swear to the great Goddess, Charlotte's timing is as bad as it comes.*

"While your magic is comparable, I suspect it requires more skill because you mimic the appearance of things around you. It's truly remarkable." It explained why Kenya had been able to disappear from view with regular cameras but remained a shadow on the one infrared he'd installed near the door of his main office.

The petite beauty's attention was focused on her hands, which were currently twisting in her lap. Nervous energy edged with exhaustion and worry swirled around her, and Bronx was anxious to get this discussion over, as well. He had other plans for his mate—plans that included exploring how perfectly her sweet body responded to his touch. Damn, she'd nearly gone up in flames earlier in the kitchen.

Knowing she burned bright when he'd tightened the pressure on her tightly peaked nipple made him more than a little anxious to further explore their connection. He hadn't planned to use magic to get the information he wanted, but it was obvious she was as anxious to share as he was to learn why she'd targeted his businesses.

Bronx suspected he knew but needed confirmation from her. Hell, the pendant around his neck hadn't stopped vibrating since the first time he'd touched her. The damned thing had still moved in slow pulses against his chest while he'd been down the hall, using the guest bathroom to shower. The movements reminded him of a tuning fork, vibrating at different frequencies depending on her proximity. Using two fingers, Bronx raised her chin as he turned her heart-shaped face, so they were eye to eye.

"Tell me why you chose my businesses to break into. There had to be others that would have better suited your needs." Her eyes widened. She might be surprised he'd been so direct, but there wasn't going to be anything she could do to resist answering honestly. The magic of a compelling voice was nearly impossible to resist unless you were also a compeller.

"I had to find you, and... well, the... pendant."

It was obvious she was fighting against the compelling magic he'd used, but he could save her the effort. Resisting required tremendous concentration and a high level of skill, and there were very few magicals who could do it successfully. Bronx could count on one hand the number of people he'd encountered who shared the skill.

He'd always known how fortunate he was to have three very distinct magical gifts. Being a shifter was fun, and he enjoyed being able to run in the moonlight, but he'd never considered it a skill since it was simply something he'd been able to do since puberty. Nonmagicals struggled with acne while he and his brothers battled spontaneous shifts until their bodies learned to control the balance between their human and wolf. Time travel was more developed, and he'd spent a lot of time learning the importance of observing but not affecting even the slightest change.

It was the use of his compelling voice that challenged him the most. Using it appropriately had been one of the hardest lessons of his youth. The ethics involved were something he and Austin discussed with their parents many times over the years since they'd both been blessed with the gift. There had been a lot of late-night conversations revolving around the consequences of their poor decisions.

Smiling to himself, Bronx remembered how appalled his mother had been to discover he'd used the magical gift on dates. Hell, he'd had more sexual encounters in high school than most men had when they graduated from college. It was one of the few times he could remember his mother being so angry, she'd raised her voice. Holy hell, she'd been off the chart pissed. Her screaming had shaken him to his core. Perhaps it wasn't her finest parenting moment, but in hindsight, he realized how effective... and necessary, it had been.

"Why did you have to find me, Kenya?" Leaning his forehead against hers, Bronx gave her a sly smile. "Tell me all of it, *Chef*. I'll know if you lie, and I want to remind you, deceiving by omission is still lying." He wanted to smile when he felt her sag against him. She wouldn't be able to lie, but there was a part of her still fighting to hide her secret.

Chapter Four

"I NEED YOUR pendant." Kenya's simple statement answered one question and begged a dozen more. Bronx knew there was a lot more to the story, so he waited. She pulled in a deep breath and sighed. Damned if he didn't almost feel sorry for her. Whatever she was going to say was a secret she desperately wanted to protect, but compelling magic made it impossible for her to keep the information to herself. "When my mom first gave the pendant to me, she told me the magic would be exponentially stronger when the two halves were reunited."

"How did you know I had the other half?" His mother hadn't given him much information before she died, but once he dug himself out of the overwhelming grief, Bronx started researching the origins of the strange symbol and the fables surrounding it.

"I didn't. I spent months reading my mother's old journals. Unfortunately, I started reading the most recent ones, those she'd been writing in before she died. Reading the books in reverse order meant it took me a long time to get to her college days." Kenya rolled her eyes, and he wondered if she was more frustrated with herself or her mother. "The first time I visited your dealership, I knew I was in the right place. You were busy filming a commercial and didn't notice me. I picked up a clipboard, and everyone assumed I was part of the crew."

"How did you cover your scent? It would have been impossible for me to overlook you if you'd ever been close enough for me to recognize you as my mate."

"I stayed upwind. My mom and I encountered shifters as we moved around the country, so I knew enough to minimize the risk. I didn't want you to be able to recognize me when I... stole the pendant."

The words were whispered so quietly, Bronx wouldn't have heard her without the enhanced hearing of a shifter. Bronx forced back his frustration. Knowing she'd intended to steal the pendant was frustrating, but it was also pathetically lame.

"Please don't be angry. I only wanted the enhanced magic to get a place to live and to fix my hearing... and maybe pay my tuition for a couple of semesters."

"Don't worry about a place to live, Chef. I know you aren't convinced, but you are my mate, and I take care of what's mine. Seeing to your safety became my number one priority the moment I recognized you." He gave her several long seconds to process what he'd said before addressing the next issue. Shifting her slight frame, so their cheeks were pressed together, he smiled when she gasped. With his lips brushing over the shell of her ear, Bronx asked, "How much do you know about the mating process, Kenya?" He felt the shiver move through her—was it a reaction to the question or the feel of his warm breath moving over the sensitive skin behind her ear? Pressing his tongue flat against her soft skin, he was gratified to feel her pulse kick up.

"Not much, really. I was too young at the time to be included in those conversations."

This close, he was beginning to pick up echoes of her thoughts, smiling to himself when she expressed frustration about her failure to read about shifters. He could save her the annoyance, but he wasn't ready to give away the perk of their growing connection. He listened as she bemoaned neglecting to do more research into the world of shifters. Romance novels might not be the best source of information, but from the way her body was responding, they probably weren't the worst either. Bronx pulled back until they were once again face to face.

"Thank you for your honesty. I know that wasn't easy for you to admit." He didn't see any reason to mention it would be nearly impossible to resist the compelling magic he'd used. This conversation was necessary for informational purposes only since she didn't have a snowball's chance in the Texas summer sun, stealing the medallion from around his neck—with or without his knowledge.

"Has your half been... ummm... reacting? I mean... well, have you noticed any difference since we met?"

He wanted to smile at the simple question. The truth was the pendant had been vibrating on and off for weeks. Now, he suspected the reaction was linked to the times she'd been nearby. He was astonished she'd managed to fly under his radar for so long when the first faint hint of the unique scent of his mate hit him like a ton of bricks earlier this evening. When the wind fully shifted, her scent had been so powerful, it was impossible to move away.

"Yes. I've never known it to react at all. It pulsed until my mother was out of sight after she gave it to me—after that, nothing. I'd always assumed it was because its energy was linked to her magic. She was a powerful witch, though most people underestimated her power."

His parents had rarely been apart for more than a few hours. It wasn't until he was in his late teens that Bronx finally understood the significance of their strong bond. Carrington Adler was descended from a long line of shifters, but his power as a magical was fed by his wife's greater gift.

"My mother's journals were filled with stories about your parents. It seems your parents and mine were friends while they were in college."

He was surprised when he felt her relax marginally when he admitted the necklace had been acting out of the ordinary. Had she thought hers was malfunctioning? *Shit, stop thinking like a damned gearhead and think like a magical, Bronx.* Tuning in to her emotions was getting easier, but after they were mated, he'd be able to get a much better read, eventually being able to hear her thoughts.

"There is one more small thing I should probably mention."

Bronx froze, his tongue pressed against the sensitive skin behind her ear as her heart rate accelerated, telling him she was afraid. Whether her fear was related to whatever she needed to share or concern about his reaction, he wasn't sure. When a shudder moved up her spine, Bronx pulled back to look into her light green eyes.

"Tell me, *Cher.*" The simple command was spoken

more as a Dom than a magical, and damned if he wasn't overjoyed when she responded immediately. Suspecting his mate was a sexual submissive when he'd first pulled her against him, Bronx was happy to find out his original assessment was accurate.

"My mother's journals were stolen." The simple statement was loaded with unspoken fear.

Bronx didn't need to ask why someone would have taken what he suspected was filled with treasured memories, as well as confidential information about members of the magical community. Information was power, and in the wrong hands, it could be deadly. His brother, Cleveland, was married to a woman whose recent exposure to the dark side's power was a wake-up call for not only the Adlers but many other magicals as well. Vienna's family harbored dark secrets that included the best and worst of the magical world.

Kenya's defeated sigh brought Bronx back to the moment. *The reluctance to share information he'd felt from her a few seconds ago had been shoved aside, replaced with something closer to grief.*

"Did the thief take anything else, *Chef?*" He watched her eyes fill with tears again, but this time she blinked them back as a surge of rage he hadn't expected rolled over him. If Bronx found the person responsible for his mate's anguish, they would pay dearly for what they'd done.

"No. I didn't really have anything else of value aside from the pendant." A thief intent on locating the two halves of the pendant would already have guessed Kenya always wore the one her mother gave her. They probably hadn't felt confident enough they could take it from her, so they'd opted to steal the journals instead.

"You're on the right track. The rumor mill in the magical community is cranked a couple of notches above frantic."

Kenya gasped at the sound of Israel's voice coming from the darkened doorway behind them. When she tried to scramble off his lap, Bronx tightened his arm around her waist, holding her tight.

"Stay where I put you, *Chef*." Turning to his brother, Bronx rolled his eyes. "You could have knocked."

"I could have, but this was more fun. If I have to drive all the way out here, my first day back from my honeymoon, I'm going to be a pain in the ass—that's just the way it works."

"Let me guess, your wife is working and told you to keep out of trouble." Shifting his attention to Kenya, Bronx added, "My new sister-in-law is Dr. Bristol Banks. She is the most popular OB/GYN in the state and absolutely brilliant—except for her taste in men."

"Fuck you. I drove over here to tell you three of your dealerships were hit tonight. It doesn't look like anyone made it past the first level of security before they heard sirens. Once I had a chance to review the tapes, I was worried." Israel cast a fleeting look at Kenya, his gaze reflecting a deep uncertainty and protectiveness, Bronx knew was coming from a place of love and loyalty rather than belief Bronx couldn't take care of himself.

Bronx's dream of having a day or two alone with Kenya before he had to expose her to the rest of his boisterous family evaporated like a gentle summer rain on a Texas sidewalk in July. Damn it all to hell and back. Standing, he set Kenya on her feet and straightened the front of the shirt she wore, buttoning all but the top button. He kissed the tip of her upturned nose before turning her to face his brother, anchoring her back to his front with an arm banded around her upper torso. No doubt, the move lifted the front hem of the shirt, but as a Dom, it was a pose Israel would recognize.

"Kenya Star, my brother, Israel. It's his security systems you've been treating as if they were little more than child's play." Israel glared at him before he schooled his expression and returned his attention to Kenya. Bronx didn't give either of them a chance to speak before continuing. "Israel, I'm pleased to introduce you to my mate." As good as his brother was at reading people and listening in on the thoughts of those he cared about, odds were he already knew, so the introduction was more for Kenya's sake than his brother's. Israel's eyes widened for a moment before a slow smile spread over this face.

"It's about fucking time you showed up." Israel tempered his harsh words with a welcoming smile. "We were starting to think the Universe couldn't find anyone to put up with him." Israel moved to stand in front of her, and Bronx felt her stiffen against him. Israel must have picked up on her fight-or-flight response because he went completely still with several feet still separating them. "Kenya, you have nothing to fear from me. If I had an issue with you, I wouldn't have shown up alone." Now it was Bronx's turn to wonder what his damned brother was thinking; fortunately, he didn't have to wait long to find out.

"I already knew who you were before I walked in." He

gave a negligent shrug, grinning when he added, "I didn't know you were my brother's mate. I'm going to give Luke a ration of shit. His facial recognition software needs a serious upgrade. It should identify future mates. All I got was your name, genealogy back a couple of generations, educational status, blood type, and shoe size." Bronx was relieved when Kenya giggled, obviously believing Israel was teasing. Unless Bronx missed his guess, his brother had indeed been given most, if not all, of the stats he'd listed.

Israel hadn't been kidding when he said he wouldn't have come alone if he'd been concerned. Hell, there were enough people in their immediate family to form a small posse. If you added in their friends and the members of Israel's security team, they could overthrow a small nation. So... the question was, why was his brother here? What could have been so damned important, he'd driven out to the lake this late? The look Israel gave him let Bronx know his brother was tuned in to his thoughts.

Yeah, yeah, I'm getting to it. Keep your damned shirt on. Pun intended since your lovely mate is almost dressed in one of your tailormade pieces. All kidding aside, Bronx, she's beautiful, but she doesn't know how much danger she's in. Israel's use of telepathic communication wasn't uncommon, but it was damned unusual for an outsider to pick up on the unspoken dialogue.

"I can't hear what you're saying, but I can feel the energy exchange, so I know you are speaking telepathically. It's the equivalent of whispering secrets behind your hand, so the nerdy kid on the playground can't tag along because no one is going to tell them where you're going." Bronx heard the underlying thread of pain in her voice and wondered how often she'd been excluded for it to be the first example she cited.

"Sorry. Kenya. Old habits and all. You have to remember, we're brothers, and we've been doing this our entire lives." The apology was short and sincere—classic Israel. "Bronx is annoyed with my intrusion, and I was assuring him I wouldn't have shown up unless it was urgent. He is demanding I get on with an explanation because he wants to be alone with you—something I totally understand."

"Now, he is stalling just to be a pain in the ass." Bronx was getting more pissed by the minute. Israel was pushing his patience past its limit. "You said Kenya is in danger. Explain. And I know you wouldn't be here if you hadn't already started working on a solution, so update us while you're at it."

This time when Israel smiled, it reached his eyes. His brother nodded his head in the direction of the bar, and Bronx fought to keep from rolling his eyes as he led Kenya to the antique monstrosity taking up one whole wall of the informal living space.

Before he'd learned how dangerous it was to interfere while time traveling, Bronx had enjoyed stashing collectibles in a warehouse. The huge brick structure was built during the early years of unprecedented industrial growth in New York. One of their ancestors built the dockside warehouse, and it remained in the family until Austin decided to move all their real estate investments to Texas. Luckily, Bronx had already been finishing up his home and was ready to move everything he'd collected out of storage. He'd found the bar in an abandoned bar in South Dakota after the onset of the California Gold Rush. The damned thing weighed over two tons, but it was a master-piece.

"This looks like something from a movie set. I have no idea how I overlooked it... holy Henry Abbott, it's amazing." Kenya ran her hand along the edge of the walnut bar, pausing over the dents and gouges. Bronx spent hours cleaning and polishing the wood, but he'd refused to erase the history by sanding away all the character.

"I'm sure my brother did a great job of distracting you when you first arrived." Israel moved behind the bar, pulling three bottles of beer from the specially made fridge and setting them on coasters. Another one of his favorite antique finds was an old soda machine with sliding top doors he'd taken to a restoration specialist in Las Vegas. His family teased him about finding the man on The Discovery Channel, but they'd changed their tune when they saw the spectacular result.

Bronx sensed the shift in Israel, so he wasn't surprised when his brother cut straight to the chase.

"Kenya, I know our mothers were friends, and I know you've been looking for the other half a magical totem—a piece everyone expects will give the owner more power than they could ever hope to accumulate any other way."

"Israel, I just learned all this. How the hell did you get it all?"

"I listened in. I'm telepathic, you know." Israel rolled his eyes, making Kenya giggle. "I also did some checking. Luke and Mitch Graysor have been tapping into every source on the damned planet, and the Council of Magic sent me a cryptic message outlining how they wanted this handled. Since the journals were stolen, it's only a matter of time before the men who have been following Kenya piece together our mother's connection. From there, they'll work their way through the siblings until they find what they're looking for."

"Oh, what have I done? By stalling, I've not only endangered Bronx, but everyone else in his family, as well." Kenya paled as she whispered the words to no one in particular. When he started to reach for her, she slid off the barstool to pace along the floor-to-ceiling windows facing his back yard. Bronx opened his mouth to reassure her, but a quick shake of Israel's head made him pause. "Why did I think I could pull this off? All this for hearing aids, a damned apartment, and a few college hours? What was I thinking? Fudge, I bet my mom is dancing around on the other side of the veil, happy as a clam, not at all worried about how badly I've mucked this up. And now the Council is involved? They'll probably lock me up in some damned dungeon and throw away the key. Of course, I guess there's a bright side... I won't need an apartment, and there won't be anything to hear but the moans and groans of people being tortured, so not having hearing aids might be a blessing."

I like her. She's going to fit in perfectly. Israel's words shifted Bronx's attention away from Kenya.

At the same time, a series of pings sounded against the windows. Both men launched themselves in Kenya's direction, but she'd already dropped to the floor by the time they made their way across the room where she'd been pacing.

Chapter Five

Kenya hadn't heard the high-pitched whine of the rifle shots, but she'd felt the vibration as they displaced the air around them. Looking up as the second and third shots hit the large window, she was shocked to see tiny shards of glass fly through the air, but the windows didn't break. Dropping to the floor when she heard the scrape of chairs over the slate tile floor, Kenya was surprised by the relief she felt when Bronx pulled her into his arms.

"I've got you, *Cher*. The windows are bulletproof, but that doesn't mean whoever is shooting couldn't have something larger in their arsenal." She could hear Israel barking orders into his phone as Bronx led her into another room. A chill raced over the surface of her skin when they stepped through a door she hadn't noticed earlier.

"This is a safe room, Kenya. We'll stay here until Israel gives us the all-clear. Several members of his team were already outside, updating the perimeter security—that's why the system was down." Running his hand through his hair in frustration, Bronx hoped she would hear the sincerity in his voice. "No one would have expected them to act so soon. I'm sure Israel thought he was staying a step ahead of them."

"Them? Who?" Her head was spinning, questions firing so quickly, it was impossible to focus on any one piece of the puzzle long enough to work out the answer.

"While you were pacing, Israel told me the security tapes outside the dealership showed two men stepping from the shadows as we drove out of the alley. He and Luke ran facial recognition on the three of you, concerned I was being set up. Your information came back immediately. Since they still hadn't gotten hits on the men, Israel wanted to fortify the perimeter and find out what he could from you." He saw her green eyes light up and wondered if she would share whatever epiphany she'd just had.

"I came into the house while you were in the shower. Big brother was using the guest bath and didn't hear the alert." Kenya didn't seem convinced Israel was telling the truth. Bronx frowned when she narrowed her eyes, clearly unconvinced he hadn't known his brother was eavesdropping.

"I know what you're thinking—you don't understand why I didn't know he was here. Kenya, I admit I wasn't focused enough to realize he'd *intruded*. Thinking about you upstairs—naked in my shower—was damned distracting. Even if I had noticed his scent, I wouldn't have thought anything about it because it's not unusual for members of my family to use my house as a base when they want to run in the woods surrounding the lake. It's safer for them to strip and leave their clothes here than it is for them to risk shifting in a public area."

She nodded, but he wasn't sure she was entirely convinced. Bronx didn't take it personally. Kenya didn't appear to have a positive history with family loyalty and trust. It would take a while for her to feel safe with him and even longer for her to trust the other members of his family.

"Will you let me watch you shift sometime? I wouldn't want to intrude, and I know we don't really know each other. If it's too much to ask, you can just tell me. I won't be offended. Sometimes, my curiosity gets me into trouble. My mom used to get really frustrated when I'd ask new people to show me their magical skills. She said it was rude, but there wasn't any other way for me to learn. We moved so many times, it's a wonder I can even read. Once I was old enough to walk to libraries, they were the first places I went to when we moved to a new town. Most librarians are awesome, and I discovered many of them are retired teachers, so that was a bonus."

Bronx listened to Kenya rattle on until she finally stopped to take a breath. Pulling her into his arms, he held her until he felt her racing heart slow, and their heartbeats synchronized. He recognized the scent of fear and hated knowing she'd lost the sense of security he'd wanted her to feel in his home. The fuckers outside were going to pay if he ever found out who they were. When she finally relaxed in his arms, Bronx pulled back to look into her eyes, sighing when he saw embarrassment clouding her expression.

"I'm sorry, that was really over the top. I don't usually panic, but it was a little unnerving, knowing someone was shooting at you." Bronx felt his eyes widen in surprise.

"Why did you think they were shooting at me, *Chef*?"

"The trajectory of the bullets was all wrong for them to have been shooting at me." He was stunned. "I could see small shards of glass flying away from the windows, so it was easy to calculate where the shots came from and their target."

It took Bronx several more minutes to get her settled enough to sit down. She drained the bottle of water he'd gotten her from the kitchenette, and he wondered if he should have given her something stronger. He was relieved when she finally took a deep breath and shrugged her shoulders.

"It's... well, you know, everything happening so fast, and I feel like I brought trouble to your door. I don't have the magical gifts you all have, but..." The door opened, and Israel stepped inside with Cameron Barnes close behind. They didn't lock the door behind them, so it was safe to assume the threat had been neutralized. Bronx had to give his brother credit, he didn't waste any time getting to the point.

"I was listening in on your conversation." Focusing his attention on Kenya, he continued, "Tell us what you know about the bullets." Holding up his hand when she hesitated, he added, "Stop. I can see the paranoia reflecting in your eyes. We're damned impressed and want to know how you were able to see the almost microscopic bits of glass dislodging from windows designed to take much more force." Cam stepped forward, his attention focused on Kenya.

"From the outside, it is almost impossible to find the damage. I'm not sure anyone would have ever found those small lines in the glass if you hadn't mentioned seeing them. Now, what we'd all like to know is how you did it." Cam Barnes swore he was retired from the CIA, but no one believed retirement was an option for an agent as skilled and highly trained as Barnes.

"Excuse me, have we met? I'm not sure why you believe I'll tell you anything."

Bronx tried unsuccessfully to suppress his chuckle at the surprise he saw flash in Cam's eyes. Typically, the only person who dared to challenge Cameron Barnes was his lovely wife and submissive, CeCe. Dr. Cecelia Barnes, a world-renowned pediatric surgeon, was only submissive to Cam—and at times, that was questionable. Cam recovered quickly, stepping forward to extend his hand to Kenya.

"You're right. I've been terribly rude. Please accept my apology." Cam introduced himself and surprised Bronx by telling Kenya he was a former agent.

Tilting her head to the side, Kenya studied Cam for several seconds before responding. "Thank you for your candor. I met your wife about a year ago." Bronx saw Cam's brows raise in surprise since he hadn't mentioned CeCe. "I helped a friend who has a street cart selling coffee outside Dr. Barnes's hospital. She was my favorite customer. Her vivacious energy was always the bright spot of my day."

Watching the change in Cam's demeanor was remarkable. Bronx doubted Kenya could have handled the situation better—three simple sentences, and she had Barnes eating out of her hand. *Hell, she should be selling cars.*

"You should have that bullet taken out of your leg. Why deal with the pain?"

Bronx sensed his mate was testing the other man, but she'd also rewarded his forthrightness with a small reveal of her own. *There is definitely more to Kenya's magic than camouflaging herself. I'm going to enjoy learning all her secrets. If she is anything like the other women in my life, it will take a lifetime.* Bronx loved his sisters—each of them so different, yet they shared so many traits, it was easy to see they were sisters. It was turning out, his sisters-in-law were no different.

"Damn, I swear, brilliant women are God's gift to the world and my private curse." It was easy to hear the respect and amusement in Cam's tone.

"I think God is onto you, Cam." Israel's taunting voice drew laughter all around. "Kenya, as much as I care about my friend's good health, my new bride has schooled me more than once on the importance of HIPPA. Don't ask me what it stands for. I only know it means nobody in the medical community is going to tell you jack shit without a signed waiver that's been notarized by three witches, a Rabbi, and a saint."

"All kidding aside, rest assured, I'll be asking you questions about the bullet at some point in the near future, but right now, I'm interested in your take on the ballistics." Cam nodded toward the door. "Let's take a walk." Bronx swallowed back his frustration as Cam led Kenya down the hall to the family room. Israel put his hand on Bronx's forearm, holding him back when Cam and Kenya stepped outside. Bronx stiffened as a growl vibrated deep in his chest.

"Calm down. I'm not trying to keep you from following your mate. I wanted you to know this situation is snowballing on us. We're meeting with Kyle and Kent tomorrow, but for now, I want you to know there were two shooters. Kenya is right—one was aiming for you. The other was positioned to take her out but didn't shoot when the first bullets bounced off the glass."

Bronx stared at his brother in disbelief. How the hell had anyone managed to get close enough with Israel's team working on the perimeter? Building a successful business taught Bronx the importance of prioritizing, so he set aside any questions that weren't solution-oriented. If it wasn't going to solve the problem at hand, set it aside for now. Learning to prioritize was one lesson he learned quickly, having recognized the mistakes his father made. It was his mission to do things differently, and he'd always been able to separate what was critical from what simply needed to be done—until now.

"Believe me, I understand—everything is different when your mate is involved and even more difficult to deal with before you can claim her. You know Kenya is safe with Cam. Hell, the man has become fucking obsessed with figuring out how magic works. The biggest threat is him questioning her until she wants to throw him in the lake." They both shook their heads, knowing the man was chasing a pipe dream. Master magicians were often several hundred years old, and most would tell you they were still learning. "I don't know how she saw the bullets or the glass slivers, but it's damned impressive." Knowing it wasn't her only magical skill made Bronx wonder how deep Kenya's magic ran and what it had to do with her mother's nomadic lifestyle.

"Let's go outside. I want to watch your mate deal with Cam. She seems to have a great head on her shoulders. Seeing her stand up to him earlier was great." Israel slapped Bronx on the shoulder as they walked out of the safe room.

"She's going to fit in great. Everyone is going to love her. Let's go see if she has any idea who was lurking in the shadows in the alley."

Chapter Six

B RONX HAD NEVER been so grateful for a thunderstorm in his entire life. Driving rain and lightning so close, it made the hair on the back of his neck stand on end was enough to send Israel and his team running for their respective cars. Cam waved as he'd sprinted to his truck, shouting something about talking to them later, but booming thunder drowned out most of his words. Luckily, he and Kenya were only a few steps from the covered patio, or they'd have been soaked for the second time.

"Don't they ever sleep? I mean, it was already late when we got here, and now it's almost morning."

"Cam doesn't sleep much. My guess is he spent too many years working black ops. I'd hate to think about the things he's seen and done. As for the rest of us, we're shifters, so we don't require as much sleep and often run most of the night." Bronx hadn't considered how the long night was affecting her. "Damn, I'm sorry. You must be exhausted. Let's get you upstairs to bed." He saw her shoulders stiffen and assumed she didn't want to sleep with him. Grasping her by the shoulders, Bronx made sure she'd settled before continuing "You can sleep anywhere you're most comfortable, *Chef*."

"Can I sleep with you? I'm not sure I'd be able to sleep in a strange place by myself. It was always so scary on the street, and I—"

Bronx cut off her need to continue, pulling her into his embrace, holding her against his chest until he felt her take a deep breath and relax in his arms. He wanted to howl at the small victory. It spoke volumes to know she'd been sleeping on the street and on sofas in his dealerships for weeks but wanted to sleep with him because she knew she'd be safe in his care.

"Let's go." Not the most eloquent or romantic response, but he could barely think, needing to feel her naked body pressed against his. When she started to climb into bed, wearing the clothes he'd given her earlier, Bronx shook his head. "No, *Cher*, we sleep naked. Strip." Her cheeks flushed deep crimson as her eyes widened in surprise when he pulled his shirt over his head and tossed it aside. His jeans were gone in seconds, and he smiled when her gaze landed on his erection.

"I…"

"*Cher*, I want you. I wouldn't deny it even if I could, but I'm not a hormonal teenager. I can control myself. We'll go at your pace. Now, come on, let's get some sleep." Pulling her bare back against his chest, Bronx wrapped his arm around her torso, making certain she'd feel safe in his arms. Kenya slowly relaxed, letting her head pillow against his bicep.

"So warm. Comfortable. Quiet. Safe." Even with his enhanced hearing, Bronx had barely been able to hear her softly spoken words. He didn't bother to respond because he'd seen her slip the hearing aids from her ears when they'd first entered the master suite. He hadn't missed the way she tried to hide the small devices behind a framed family picture he kept on a chest of drawers.

Her physical challenge didn't mean anything to him, and he needed to make that clear sooner rather than later. He had several employees who were hearing impaired. His company made every accommodation they could, and they'd always been rewarded with talented and loyal partners. He doubted she knew all the physical benefits of being claimed, but she'd learn soon enough. All of her senses would sharpen, but her eyesight and hearing would be the most noticeable. Even the human mates who were never able to shift were shocked about the changes to those two senses. Most claimed mates gained a shifter's ability to heal rapidly and swore it was one of the best changes they experienced.

"I can almost hear you thinking. You told me to relax and rest, but you aren't doing the same. Is there something I should know… a problem no one has mentioned?"

"No, *Chef*, I won't keep anything from you when your safety is at stake." Moving his hand to cup the underside of her bare breast, Bronx brushed his calloused thumb over her nipple, enormously pleased when she gasped, arching into his touch. The nub tightened, and he vowed to visit the back room at Catalina's jewelry shop to find the perfect pair of nipple clamps. "I was thinking about all the physical enhancements non-shifters experience when they are claimed."

He wasn't surprised when she turned to face him.

Reading lips was probably something she'd been doing for so long, it was as essential to her ability to hear as her aids. Bronx was glad he'd left one of the bedside lamps on—he hadn't wanted her to wake up disoriented because it was an unfamiliar place. Now, the soft light was going to work to her advantage in a way he hadn't anticipated. Knowing she needed to see his face, he allowed her to put a small amount of distance between them.

"Even though I hear men's voices better than I hear women, I still need to be able to see you." It wasn't hard to see how much the admission cost her, and he didn't want her to feel any embarrassment, so he took full advantage of the change in their positions and kissed her.

"*Cher*, I'm happy to do whatever makes it easier for you."

"You said something about physical enhancements. Please tell me you weren't talking about big boobs because I'd have to buy all new clothes. Not that I have many clothes, but I don't have any money either, so it all works out in a twisted sort of way. I'd probably have to relearn how to walk, too. All in all, I'm not sure what I'd do with big breasts." For a couple of seconds, Bronx was too stunned to speak, unsure if she was kidding or suffering from some sort of post-traumatic stress episode. When he saw the corners of her mouth tip up, Bronx pinned her beneath him and chuckled.

"You didn't think I was going to catch-on, did you?" Her smile spread until her eyes were dancing with mischief. "Oh, *Cher*, I will enjoy sparring with you. My sisters have trained me well. I've always been miles ahead of my brothers when it came to matching wits with their left of center senses of humor." Leaning down, he circled the tight buds of her nipples with the tip of his tongue before blowing cool air over both damp tips and watching them tighten into peaks so stiff, he knew they were throbbing in need.

Bronx suspected Kenya would enjoy the small bite of pain a pair of adjustable clips would give her. He'd spent years helping train subs and rarely met one who started classes believing she'd enjoy pain. Showing newbies how exhilarating walking the fine line between pleasure and pain could be was one of his favorite parts of submissive training. During his last couple of years, his businesses had grown so fast, Bronx didn't have enough free time to commit to being a trainer, but he hadn't forgotten the lessons.

"I should probably apologize for teasing you, but I hate to set a precedent. No sense in starting that nonsense, or I'd be stuck doing it forever. Sooner or later, you're bound to figure out what a dork I am, so what's the point? If you stick around long enough, you're going to find out about my weird my sense of humor, anyway." Bronx had to remind himself that even though she'd met a few shifters, it was obvious she didn't know much about them.

"Shifters mate for life, *Chef*. We commit ourselves fully to the one person fate chooses for us. *Sticking around* is a given."

"What if... well, what if it turns out you don't want the mate fate chose for you?"

"Fate doesn't make mistakes, *Chef*." She didn't seem

convinced, but he would add it to the list of things she'd learn after he claimed her. The melding of the DNA would not only change her physically, it would also open up her mind to a new level of understanding. He would also experience important changes, including the ability to easily read her emotions and hear her thoughts. He'd also be able to track her anywhere in the world, and it would be impossible for her to hide or be hidden from him.

"Everybody always seems to change their mind, you know, insisting they'll stay, but then they don't." She was looking over his shoulder, and he recognized the far-away look in her eyes.

Kenya was lost in painful memories, and as much as he hated seeing the forlorn expression, he needed to know as much about her as possible. He'd seen submissives go completely off the rails when a Dom unintentionally stepped on an emotional landmine. Those triggers were powerful, and more often than not, the submissive wasn't even aware of their existence.

"I never knew my dad. My mom said he left us not long after I was born. She told me the only reason she stayed around was because she didn't have anyone to leave me with. I think she was afraid of someone, but I didn't know who. The only thing she ever truly loved was drugs." Letting out a breath, Bronx doubted she realized she was holding, he suspected she was trying to settle her emotions before continuing. Shifting her gaze back to meet his, she gave him a small smile that didn't reach her eyes. "Don't get me wrong; it wasn't all bad. She could be a lot of fun when she was high or *in love*." He certainly didn't miss the sarcasm in her voice as she drew out the last two words.

"When I got older, I recognized her infatuation with men for what it was—she used them for money and a good time, then when the cash flow dwindled, and the relationship became stale, she'd pack up, and we'd slip away... usually in the middle of the day when the guy was at work. You know, a couple of them were nice guys. One even offered to let me stay, so I didn't have to change schools, but she wouldn't even discuss it." Bronx could hear the pain in her voice, and as much as he wanted to pull her close to offer comfort, he wanted her to know she could share concerns without him jumping in.

One of the most valuable lessons his older sister, Asia, taught him was the power of listening. He'd tried to give a high school girlfriend some much-needed advice on a problem she was having with a teacher. The girl had promptly dumped him, and Bronx had been baffled. He'd been sitting at the kitchen bar late that night, bemoaning the situation to Asia. She'd shaken her head and looked at him as if he was the dumbest man on the planet.

"Girls don't want you to solve their problems—hell, most of them already know the answer, or at the very least, they know all the options. They just want you to listen while they sort it out for themselves." She gave him a short lesson in what she called the art of asking thoughtful questions before giving him a hug and walking away.

Asia had bounded up the stairs in their family's home in Austin, taking them two at a time, shouting over her shoulder that she expected an extra-special Christmas gift when she returned for her semester break in a couple of months. He'd made certain she had it, too. Luckily, Catalina started designing high-end pieces before she'd even started high school. Her inventory was always impressive, and he'd found a diamond and sapphire bracelet he knew Asia still wore regularly.

KENYA KNEW SHE was talking too much. Damn it all to hopscotch, why was she telling Bronx things she'd never confessed to anyone? She knew the answer, but it was hard to admit how good it felt to *be heard*. She'd spent so much of her life trying desperately to be invisible, it shouldn't surprise anyone that blending into her surroundings was the one magic skill she'd always found easiest. Her mom insisted Kenya's magic came from her side of the family, but after reading her mom's journals, she'd learned that was simply one more lie added to a very long list.

"I'm sorry... I feel like I'm unloading a lot of baggage on your doorstep. You probably wish you'd never brought me home with you. Someone tried to shoot you, for heaven's sake. I'll bet that's never happened before. A couple of hours with me, and you've already got a target painted on your back."

"*Stop.*" The sharp tone of his voice made her jerk her eyes back to his. She'd been speaking to him, but the truth was, she'd been so lost in her own thoughts, she'd almost forgotten he was close enough to hear even the softest whispers. "There were two shooters. Israel said they believe the second was planning to shoot you, but after seeing the first bullets bounce off the glass, they both fled."

She was chewing on her lip, and he almost smiled. If he'd just wait, her inherent honestly would kick in, and she'd confess Cam had already told her about the second gunman—in *three, two, one...*

"Mr. Barnes said there was another person closer to the river, but I thought he was just fishing for information." This time, Bronx wasn't able to hold back his smile and chuckle.

"*Cheŕ*, Cam Barnes is honest to a fault. He doesn't fish, and he walked in here knowing more about you than you can possibly imagine."

"How do you know that?"

"Because I know Cam, and I know my brother. They don't go into situations unprepared if they can avoid it, and they had plenty of time to pull together a mountain of information about you. Once your face pinged the facial recognition program, they would have had pages and pages of information before they finished their after-dinner drinks."

IT WAS TRUE the man had seemed to know a lot about her, but she hadn't thought to wonder why until now. Damn, she'd always tried to fly under the technology radar. Looking for the other half of the pendant had been her sole focus, and she hadn't wanted to leave a digital trail. Being able to hear and have a place to live had been all she'd focused on for months.

She wanted to be able to dance to music again. Not being able to hear children playing in the park was gut-wrenching, and having people look at her like she was dumber than a box of rocks when her response was clearly off-base made her feel ignorant. Answering the questions she thought they'd ask almost always caused so much confusion, she'd finally stopped engaging in even the most casual conversations.

"What was that thought?"

"What?"

"That last thought. What was it? And don't bother lying because I'll know."

She could feel the connection between them growing and didn't doubt he'd know if she gave him anything less than a truthful answer. Hell's tiny tinkling bells, she was too tired to make up a plausible fib, anyway. Telling him how isolating her hearing impairment had become was a relief. At least now, if he asked her a question and her answer seemed to come from the farthest corner of left field, he'd understand why.

"I have several employees who have told me the same thing. A couple of them confided their hearing loss was responsible for more than one failed relationship. Dating often involves conversations in noisy environments—restaurants, bars, theaters, ballparks, etc. Their hearing loss made those chats impossible." She nodded.

"It's awful, and hearing aids are a nightmare in those places because they magnify *everything*. This close... in a quiet room, I can almost pretend I'm like everyone else."

"*Cheŕ*, you are not like anyone else, and that's exactly as it should be. Remember, we are fated mates—uniquely perfect for one another." She felt her eyes fill with tears at his sweet words and hoped he could see her gratitude because she wasn't sure it would be possible to speak around the lump in her throat. "Fatigue is coming off you in waves, *Chef*."

She knew he was going to insist she go to sleep, but all she could think about was how wonderful it would feel to have this man touch her—to show her the pleasure she'd only read about in books. Before she could reconsider, she leaned forward and brushed her hips over his.

"Please."

To his credit, Bronx didn't appear frustrated with her bold move. His gaze softened, his pupils dilating until there was only a narrow ring of color visible. She wasn't sure what she was asking for, but he seemed to understand. He didn't respond immediately, continuing to watch her with such intensity, Kenya started to become uncomfortable. Maybe she'd overstepped some boundary or broken some unspoken rule.

"We're going to have to work on your focus, *Chef*. I'm looking forward to testing your limits and showing you more pleasure than you ever dreamed possible. The only thing I want more than I want to make love to you is to claim you as my mate. Put yourself in my hands, Kenya. Tell me you understand what I want from you. This is too important for there to be any misunderstandings between us. I don't want you to feel pressured, and I damned well don't want you to wake up tomorrow regretting what's about to happen here."

She was beginning to think he was going to talk her to death. Fudgesicles in paradise, maybe this was his way of sidestepping. Maybe he was reconsidering—not like she'd be surprised. Who wants to bed a woman who brings snipers into their life? The whole thing was starting to lose its appeal, and for a moment, she wondered if that was the plan.

"You're reading too much into what I said, Kenya. I don't want to assume you want me to fuck you into a stupor if that wasn't what you had in mind."

Fuck-a-dilly circus. Nothing like laying it right out there for the whole world to see. Why, oh, why had she ever thought she could keep up with this man? But then again, who better to learn from than a man who so clearly had so much more experience?

"I want you to touch me. Sleeping next to you would be great, but it isn't going to be enough." She tried to slow her breathing before she passed out. "Damn, I thought it was supposed to be women who always wanted to talk, and that was after sex, right? So, this whole conversation is throwing me off a little. Do I fully understand what you want from me? Probably not. I don't have enough experience with men and certainly not any with a Dominant. I don't think reading *Fifty Shades of Gray* counts as experience—maybe if I'd seen the movies, too." Shaking her head in an effort to bring her thoughts back to the topic at hand.

"Fucking hell," Bronx practically growled the words as he pinned her beneath him and slanted his lips over hers. Her back arched involuntarily, pressing her breasts against his chest, letting his hair tease her nipples. A wave of desire built deep in her core, sending lightning racing up and down her spine, each strike sending a jolt of electrified need directly to her pussy.

Her vagina clenched, and Kenya wanted him to do

something… anything to satisfy the aching need burning her from the inside out. Nothing existed but the man pressed against her. When she felt his cock's rigid length pressing against her mound, Kenya's legs parted of their own volition. Feeling the smooth skin covering the head of his cock sliding through her wet folds made her wish she could tilt her hips, but he held her still.

"We were only going slow until you agreed to be mine. Now, I set the pace, Cher."

Fudgesicles, get on with it already… before I burst into flames.

Chapter Seven

BRONX WASN'T SURE which body part was going to melt-down from need first—his cock or his brain. Every minute he spent with his mate solidified their connection, and he hadn't even formally claimed her yet. *Fuck me seven ways to Sunday, if it gets better than this, I may not survive.*

"Are you ready for me, *Chef*? Is your pussy slick with cream, waiting for me to push in so deep, we'll both lose our minds?" Her earthy scent surrounded him, and Bronx was glad he'd insisted she slept naked. Knowing his cock wouldn't encounter any obstacle made her so tempting, he was struggling to control the urge to fuck her with all the urgency and passion boiling in his blood.

Fate not only chose a shifter's mate, the Universe also bestowed a sexual attraction so strong, it was recognized as a rite of passage. Many packs sheltered newly mated couples or polys for several weeks after their mating, knowing they were completely and utterly focused on fucking. Meals were delivered to their suite, and pack betas covered for their Alpha until he'd worked it out of his system and could once again focus on pack business.

Bronx circled the tip of his cock around her opening,

groaning as agonized pleasure ripped through him. Surprise sifted through the sexual fog clouding his brain when Kenya's legs opened further, and his tip finally found its mark. Heat spread over the sensitive skin covering his cock head as he worked his way inside, his progress slowed by the vice-like grip of her vaginal muscles.

"Damn, *Cher*, you are so tight. How long has it been for you?" He felt her entire body tense beneath him and knew he'd asked a question she didn't want to answer. "It's important for you to be honest with me, Kenya. I don't want to hurt you. I'm not a small man, and you're not only petite, your pussy is as tight as a—" Before he could finish the sentence, he heard what sounded too much like a strangled sob. Pulling back so he could see her face, Bronx knew she'd never been taken by a man.

"I haven't actually ever... well, I haven't had real sex." *Real sex? As opposed to pretend sex?* "That didn't sound right, did it? What I mean is, I had a boyfriend who put his fingers inside me once. I wasn't impressed. I kept reading about how great it would feel, but it hurt."

Bronx was shocked by her admission. It was humbling to admit how pleased he was he'd be the first man to push himself into her slick heat. Damn, he was dying to fuck her every way imaginable, to hear her scream his name as her mind shattered from pleasure. It would be his great honor to erase the memory of discomfort some fumble-fingered kid.

"We'll go slow. If you feel anything other than a pleasurable burn, tell me. I don't want to tear the tender tissues of your vagina." He didn't want to hurt her, and he damned well didn't want to do anything that would keep them from a repeat performance or two during the night.

"Yes, I promise. Can we skip some of the tutorial and get back to the learn as you go part?" Bronx felt himself smiling and couldn't remember the last time a woman had amused him during sex. He'd only played at the club a few times during the past couple of years because his business had taken over his life. "I'm on the pill, and since I haven't ever had... umm, you know."

"Real sex?" Bronx tried to temper the amusement in his voice but knew he'd failed when he saw her eyes sparkle with mock annoyance.

"Are you laughing at me? Because it seems pretty rude to laugh at someone when your favorite appendage is prodding your target."

"Point well-made, Cher. It would be foolish to risk my cock's safety for a cheap joke. I have plans—many, many plans—for my... what did you call it? Oh yeah, favorite appendage." This time, barely visible laugh lines creased the corners of her eyes, and Bronx silently vowed to make certain those shallow wrinkles became more pronounced every day. He'd always believed the most beautiful women were those who smiled easily and often. Spotting happy couples walking into his dealerships was a skill he developed early. All he had to do was look for those who had character lines drawn deep around their eyes because those were the pairs who laughed together.

Bronx pushed the head of his cock in until the walls of her vagina tightened around him with a vice-like grip. "Relax, Cher, let me in, I promise you'll not regret it." She gave a clipped nod as the energy surrounding her seemed to shift from guarded to desire. Bronx was determined to make certain this was a moment she would remember forever with fondness. He would take his time—no matter how excruciating it was to hold back. By the time he was balls deep in heaven, they were both slick with sweat.

"Feeling your body pulse around my cock is the sweetest torture. The walls of your channel trying to pull me deeper is the hottest thing I've ever experienced." His tip was already pressed against her cervix, her sweet gasp every time he flexed all the proof he needed, she was attuned to the pleasure awaiting her.

"More. Please. Just because I haven't done this doesn't mean my body doesn't want to chase it. It feels like a wave, building slowly, and the crest will be epic if I can just hang on long enough."

Bronx was genuinely surprised by her insight. He'd never wanted to be a woman's first because he'd understood the inherent responsibility and wanted to avoid having a woman other than his mate intimately bound to him. Everything was different with Kenya. Introducing her to the pleasure of submission was going to be the icing on a very sweet cake.

"I'm going to give you what you need." He was thrilled to find out she needed something more to push her over the edge. Plain vanilla sex would leave her wanting. Thank the Great Goddess above for sending him a mate who needed his dominance as much as he needed her submission. Wrapping his hands around her wrists, Bronx pulled her hands over her head, guiding her fingers to the steel posts of his headboard. "Hold on. Don't let go, or I'll stop."

Her eyes widened as her slender fingers encircled the smooth metal.

"There are only three acceptable responses, *Cheŕ*, do you know what they are?" Without waiting for her to answer, Bronx forged ahead. "*Yes, Sir* is always preferable. Stating your answer in a simple, respectful way ensures there are fewer opportunities for misunderstandings. If you are unsure, saying *yellow* will let me know we need to pause so you can ask questions. Think of it as a highway caution light. If something is too much for you to bear, physically or emotionally, saying the word *red* will stop everything."

"Forever?" It was a common newbie question and one he should have anticipated.

"No, *Cheŕ*. Everything stops until we've had time to discuss what went wrong and how we can avoid making a similar mistake in the future." Every Dom he knew would delay another scene until the next day, but there wasn't any reason to overwhelm her with details. "If you're honest, in your answers and responses, there won't be a reason for you to use a safe word. Do you understand? I know it was a crash course." He'd be able to read her body's responses if she didn't deliberately mask them.

"Yes, Sir. I trust you. I've been studying you for months, and I've seen how you treat people."

Bronx nodded, grateful for the gift of her trust. He looked at her hands and shook his head when he saw the death grip she had on the bed. Prying her fingers loose, he gently massaged them before putting them back in place.

"I don't want you to cut off your circulation. I've asked

you to hold on, so you stay in place because I want this to last, and *Chér*, if you touch me, it will be over too soon." Bronx was pleased to see her smile. He set a slow pace, giving her time to fully adjust to his size and the inevitable stretch as blood rushed to her sex, swelling the tissues. The extra time also let his cock ready itself for what he was sure was going to be an earth-shattering climax.

"Oh, my stars and garters, it's so much better than I imagined."

He agreed. Her body was already starting to quake around him, the intensity of her response pushing him closer and closer to his own release. Bronx wasn't sure what pushed him more—his wolf's physical desire for his mate or the sudden pressure in his chest from an emotion he'd never experienced with another woman during sex.

"I wanted to make slow, sensuous love to you, Kenya—show you how perfect it would be once we were mated—but you are shredding my control, *Chér*."

"Faster. Please. Sir."

Any question he'd had about Kenya being able to embrace her inner submissive shattered into a splintered memory. Bronx was torn between giving her what she asked for and playing it safer than he knew was warranted. The sound of her soft whimpers as her body locked down around him snapped the last thread of his control.

"Fuck me. Ride it out *Chér*. Stay with me until you've milked the last drop." He thrust until fire raced up his spine, exploding at the base of his skull, then rocketing back down to boil in his groin. The first spurts of cum felt like his testicles were being squeezed in a damned juicer.

For a few seconds, Bronx wondered if he'd ever catch his breath. By the time he was spent, they were both panting for breath, and it was several seconds before he had it together enough to roll to his side. He wanted to stay buried inside her for as long as possible, every moment strengthening the bond between them. It wasn't as good as claiming her, but it was still an important part of the process.

"I'll get a warm cloth for you as soon as I'm sure my legs won't crumple out from under me, *Cheŕ*."

"I can clean myself up if you'll just let me rest for a second or two." She sucked in a deep breath, and for a few seconds, he thought she was going to pull away. Kenya finally let out a deep sigh as if she'd admitted a huge defeat. "Okay, it seems as though it's going to be a little longer than I originally planned. My brain doesn't seem to be speaking to my muscles at the moment." As amused as he was by her observation, he wasn't going to change his plan.

"Part of my privilege and responsibility as your Dom and mate is to see to your comfort and safety. Don't think for a minute, I intend to give up the opportunity to pamper you." He understood her reluctance. She'd been on her own for a long time—hell, if he had to guess, he'd put his money on her taking on the role of *parent* for her mother more often than it was the other way around. Nothing he'd heard or read indicated Lisa Star had ever been a candidate for mother of the year.

Pulling her close once again and wrapping her in his embrace, Bronx sent up a silent prayer of gratitude he'd finally found her—and for the bulletproof glass his family insisted he install when he'd built his home. The questions about their parents' accident had never been answered, and since the rumor mill continued to churn, despite the years that had passed, it hadn't seemed extreme.

The youngest of his siblings had been the only one who gave Austin a hard time about security. Paris tried to evade her oldest brother's security net while she was in college, but it hadn't worked. Austin hadn't been the only one responsible for keeping tabs on the little hellion, but he'd been the one she blamed. Paris's rebellion of choice was speeding, and the irony of her marrying a sheriff, who she met when he'd pulled her over for speeding, wasn't lost on anyone. As far as Austin was concerned, it was a sweet bit of karma, and knowing the man was a strict Dom was an added bonus. His position might help keep Paris in line, but no one believed she would ever be the poster child for safe driving.

By the time he returned to the bed, Kenya was fast asleep. She barely stirred as he wiped his seed from the inside of her thighs and the swollen folds of her sex. Patting the tender tissues dry, Bronx smiled to himself, knowing he'd marked her in a way no other man ever could. Settling next to her, Bronx pulled his phone from the nightstand and started reading the file Israel sent earlier. The more he read, the more suspicious he became. There were too many similarities between Kenya's story and Israel's wife, Bristol's. Small details echoed of familiarity, making the hair on the back of Bronx's neck stand on end.

It's damned unsettling, isn't it? If you add in what we know about Denali and Vienna, things get even dicier. Bronx was surprised to see the text pop up at the top of his phone's small screen. Israel didn't usually bother messaging when he could speak telepathically. *I was afraid I'd disturb your sleeping mate. She seemed sensitive to the electrical energy... this seemed safer.* Bronx didn't believe in coincidence and knew his brother was an even bigger skeptic.

There are too many similarities for it to be chance. I assume you've already forwarded this to everyone who'll be at the meeting at Prairie Winds. It was a statement rather than a question, but he still wanted his brother's assurance others would have time to run their own background checks. It would be unlike Israel to miss something, but Bronx wasn't willing to take a chance, and he knew Israel would enlist every available resource when it came to Bristol's safety.

Austin sent a message to the Council of Magic. He believes this is a larger issue than any of us realize, and I've learned to trust his intuition. A shudder of worry worked its way up Bronx spine.

Where is Cat? For some reason, his sister's face flashed through his mind. He wasn't sure it meant anything, but at this point, he didn't want to take any chances.

On a plane. She's looking for Cooper. Cam has people shadowing her, and no, she doesn't know. She'll be pissed as hell when she figures it out. My mate is home. Don't be late for the meeting.

Bronx smiled at the screen as it faded to black. There wasn't any reason to say goodbye. Israel was already gone, his attention now completely centered on Bristol—as it should be. Bronx couldn't remember ever seeing his brother as happy as he'd been since Dr. Bristol Banks came into his life.

Setting his phone aside, Bronx pulled Kenya close and

waited for their heartbeats to synchronize. He'd read how settling it was when mate's bodies were aligned as one, but he hadn't been fully prepared for the sense of peace he felt with her in his arms. When her breathing slowly settled into the same restful rhythm of his own, Bronx let himself drift into a light sleep. Until he was certain she was safe, he wasn't sure he'd be able to sleep soundly.

Welcome to my world. His brother's words drifted lightly through his mind, the last thing he remembered before sleep claimed him.

Chapter Eight

KENYA FELT HER eyes widened as they drove through an impressive set of security gates so large, she doubted they could be opened by hand. Looking ahead, she was stunned to see a tree-lined driveway wider than most of the streets in Austin.

"It's beautiful."

"Not what you expected?" Bronx smiled at her as they made their way down the long drive.

She knew he'd been enormously pleased to find dozens of shopping bags filled with clothing sitting outside the bedroom door when they'd gotten up a couple of hours earlier. His family's generosity was so over the top, she had trouble wrapping her head around it. Kenya had been so overcome with emotion, she'd been rendered speechless—not something that happened often. Pulling the garments from the bags, she'd become more overwhelmed with each new piece. Tugging nervously at the hem of her new dress, Kenya wanted to pinch herself to be absolutely certain she wasn't dreaming.

"Stop fidgeting, *Chef*. You look beautiful... the dress is nice, too." He winked at her as he pulled the car to a stop in front of a set of stone steps leading to a massive pair of doors. She watched him pull a small remote from his pocket, her entire body responding before he had a chance to press the small button she knew would light her up from the inside out. "I do love the way your body responds, *Cher*. That little bullet vibrator won't be a secret for long if you flush at the sight of the remote. There isn't a Dom in the world who wouldn't recognize that look."

"You already showed me how effective the small devil-blessed device can be. Perhaps you'd like to wait until we're alone again before giving it another go?" She knew the answer before she asked, the gleam in his eyes telling her how much he enjoyed playing with her.

"The club might not be open, but I can assure you the people waiting for us inside are experienced sexual dominants, several with extensive special forces experience. *Cher* these men don't miss even the smallest nuance. They'll be watching you closely, even if you don't notice their scrutiny. I want to control what they see." She suddenly understood what he was doing. If they were focused on her sexual responses, they might not push her to the point she wanted to fade.

The door opened as they started up the stairs. Two men who looked so much alike, she wondered if anyone could tell them apart, stepped out onto what had to be the largest porch she'd ever seen.

"Tobi and Gracie are out that door." One of the men Bronx introduced as Kent and Kyle West waved his hand toward an open door at the back of the room. "They're working on a new Christmas display. They've helped set up forum shops in clubs all over the country and often design displays to sell as part of their marketing services."

"Damn, Kyle, maybe I'll tell the ladies they should hire you as a spokesman." At least now she knew the ornery one was Kent.

"Piss off. I didn't want Kenya to walk outside and see... well, hell, who knows what?"

"I suppose your explanation did sound more professional than, *they're outside trying to figure out how to make a well-endowed blow-up man look like Santa.*" The first man rolled his eyes before recentering his attention on Bronx.

"See what I have to deal with? I swear your parents were brilliant—having more than two children dilutes the time you are forced to spend with any one of your siblings."

"You're lucky we were twins, at least you had one friend in school." She noted the amusement in the second man's eyes and assumed this was a well-rehearsed way for them to put other people at ease, particularly those they were trying to figure out.

Kenya was beginning to see small differences between the two men. At first, she hadn't been able to tell them apart, but now, their personalities helped distinguish one from the other.

Kent West winked, adding, "Never mind him, we told the ladies you were coming, so they're working on the patio rather than their office in one of the back buildings." Before she could respond, Bronx turned her away from the others.

"I won't be long, *Chef*. You'll enjoy Tobi and Gracie's company. I'm sure they've been briefed, so you won't have to scrutinize everything you say. You can trust Tobi and Gracie. They are wild as the wind but loyal as any friend you'll ever find."

Kenya took a deep breath and nodded. She and her mother had never lived anywhere long enough for her to make real friends. She walked inside with the men, then followed their directions into the main room. Walking to the club's back door seemed to take forever, but she finally took a tentative step outside and gasped.

Two women stood shoulder to shoulder, facing a large, very well-endowed, (mostly) inflated man.

"I told you this plastic wasn't thick enough."

"Yeah, yeah. What I don't understand is why the rest of him is going soft, but his cock is still pumped up. What's up with that?" The petite blonde leaned forward, giving the inflatable man's cock a firm smack. They all three watched—intrigued and amused as it bounced up and down.

"No clue. It sure doesn't work that way at my house." The woman with long dark hair laughed as she tilted her head to the side. "Can't see my men being thrilled about the idea of having their dicks smacked like that either."

"Men... go figure. All Mr. Rough and Tough until it comes to their favorite appendage."

Hearing the woman refer to a man's cock as his favorite appendage made Kenya snicker, the noise alerting the women to her presence. Spinning around, both women gave her welcoming smiles, quickly introducing themselves. Turning back to the plastic man, they all watched in fascinated horror as he slowly melted away—within seconds, Mr. Naked Plastic was in a puddle, his impressive cock the last thing to deflate.

"I'm not sure what I find the most appalling, the fact I paid eighty dollars for it or that we all three watched its sad demise like it was the most interesting thing we've ever seen." Tobi's eyes never left the plastic man, shaking her head in disgust.

"Darling daughter, is there something you need to share? I could have their father talk to the boys. If things have gotten to this point, we might need to call in an expert or two."

Kenya turned to find a stunning middle-aged woman standing nearby, her mischievous grin a sure sign her sense of humor made her as beautiful on the inside as she was on the outside. Quick introductions were made, and the four of them moved to a shaded area for lemonade.

"Lilly, I'm so glad you are home. I'm not sure who missed you the most, Kodi, Kameron, or me."

"It was a fun trip. Blowing up stuff is invigorating." Kenya stared at the other woman in disbelief. She'd read stories in the society news about Lilly West, never dreaming she'd have the opportunity to meet the pillar of Texas society in person. She turned her attention to Kenya and grinned. "Bronx's brother, Kensington, invited me to visit the set of a movie he's working on in Mexico. I stayed an extra day to visit a crystal mine with Denali. Did you know those mines generate their own heat? Crispy critters, it was like an oven in there." Kenya knew her eyes must have reflected her interest when Lilly chuckled.

"You and Denali are two peas in a pod. She was so excited about visiting the mine, she was practically bouncing up and down during the entire drive out to the site. I didn't think it was something I would enjoy, but she wanted to go so badly, and the men had something without explosives planned, so I figured what the hell." Reaching forward, Lilly's blue eyes lightened in curiosity as she lifted Kenya's pendant, studying it closely before frowning. The woman's dark hair and blue eyes were a striking contrast, but that wasn't what made her beautiful—it was the vivacious energy Kenya could feel swirling around her. There was a light inside her Kenya recognized and felt drawn to.

"What an interesting... coincidence." Lilly seemed genuinely confused as she studied the magical symbol.

"What are you talking about, Mom?"

Kenya looked up, surprised to find a semi-circle of men surrounding them. *Holy hell, where did they all come from?*

"Darlin', what is it about Kenya's pretty necklace that's caught your attention?" The older men who looked like Kent and Kyle regarded Lilly with affection. Kenya had to look twice because the man and the one standing beside him looked exactly alike. Bronx had warned her poly relationships were common at Prairie Winds. Kenya found the idea interesting but knew it wasn't something she'd be interested in. *Okay, these must be Kent and Kyle's fathers. Is that even possible? Geez, I really need to start reading up on this stuff.*

"That's a pretty piece; it reminds me of one I saw recently." The second man was focused on Kenya's pendant rather than his wife. "Hmmm, now let me think. Oh, yes, it was when we stopped by Austin and Charlotte's to see the new baby, there was a framed piece hanging above Marshall's crib. It wasn't exactly the same, but it was damned close. I'm not an artisan, but even I know it must have been made by the same person."

"Charlotte said it was a protection symbol her grand-mother gave her shortly before she died. After Austin collared her, she decided to frame it for the nursery." The two older men seemed lost in their own conversation, but Kyle's attention never wavered from his mother.

Kenya was struggling to keep up with so many unfamiliar voices. Her hearing aids weren't the most advanced on the market, and even though they amplified sound, it was still difficult to figure out where the sound was coming from.

"Stop." The booming voice of a man towering over everyone else brought instant silence. "You all know Kenya is hearing impaired, yet you are talking over each other and muttering. You're making it impossible for her to keep up." Turning his attention to her, his stern expression cleared as a warm smile completely transformed his appearance. It was only then Kenya noticed his hand was resting on Gracie's shoulder.

"We haven't been introduced yet, Kenya. I'm Jax McDonald. My wife and I have both worked with the hearing impaired, and I want you to signal one of us if the conversation gets out of hand again. It's too important to know what's happening for you to be excluded from the discussion."

A wave of gratitude threatened to swamp her, a lump forming in her throat. Feeling the warmth of Bronx's hand when he settled it on top of her shoulder grounded her in a way she hadn't expected. The quiet show of support was enough to pull her back from the emotional edge.

"Damn. We need to step up our game, people. We're

better than this. Speak clearly and make certain Kenya is able to see you when you're talking to her." Kent West put his words into practice, then gave her a thumbs up.

"Jax is right. This is too important for there to be any miscommunication. Mom, tell me why the pendant caught your attention." Tobi stood up quickly, turning to give her husband a big hug and doing the same to Kent before returning to her seat. Leaning close to Kenya, Tobi did the worst stage whisper in history.

"They are so getting laid. I'm sending the kids to their grandparents tonight." The entire group erupted in laughter, and Kenya was grateful for the break in the tension.

"Kitten, I swear you are going to be the death of me." Kyle's voice was thick with sarcasm.

"Maybe so, brother, but what a way to go." Kent leaned down to waggle his eyebrows at his lovely wife. "You're on, Sweetness. I'm looking forward to spending some time alone with you."

"Could you two focus for a hot minute? Jesus, Joseph, and Mary." Jax shook his head at what Kenya suspected was a common occurrence.

"Denali was wearing a similar symbol when we toured the mine. It wasn't exactly the same as this one or Charlotte's, but it was obviously made by the same person. A man at the mine seemed extremely interested in it—unusually so. We stopped at a local café for dinner before making the drive back to the hotel. As we walked back to the car, a man wearing a mask stepped from the shadows and demanded our purses and jewelry. I started to comply but realized he was solely focused on Denali. His gaze zeroed in on her necklace."

"Knowing Denali, it didn't end well for him." It was the first time Israel had spoken, and Kenya noted the affection she heard in his voice.

"She laughed at him, but when we started to walk around him, the jerk pulled a knife on us." When Lilly's husbands both stepped forward, their postures shifting instantly from casual amusement to worried protectors, but she waved them off. "Honestly, that young woman moved so fast, I couldn't begin to tell you what she did. All I know is by the time I blinked twice, Denali had the knife, and the masked man was a moaning heap on the sidewalk."

"Did you get a good look at the knife, Mrs. West?" A man in a dark suit with narrow stripes stepped up to the table. His deep, rich voice seemed odd coming from a man Kenya thought must be pushing eighty. The thought had no sooner raced through her mind than she heard Israel cough in the worst cover-up of laughter in the history of phony. The man turned his attention to her, his dark eyes sparkling with mischief. Something about him put her at ease. She'd never known either of her grandfathers, but this man was what she'd always imagined hers would have looked like.

"Sweetheart, I cannot begin to tell you how flattered I am your imagination sees me as your grandfather. I'll be happy to tell my granddaughter she has to share me with her new sister-in-law." Kenya felt her face heat when he gave her a saucy wink. "You and I will be having a chat about family one day in the future, but right now, I'm trying to track down some very important artifacts." When the older man returned his attention to Lilly, Bronx leaned down to explain.

"The man who just agreed to be your surrogate grandfather is the head of the Council of Magic. Audric Stafford is also Charlotte Adler's grandfather." Bronx's warm breath moving against the shell of her ear made her pussy clench with need, and she prayed he didn't decide this was a good time to activate the device she suddenly remembered was resting silently deep in her core.

My need for his touch is growing stronger. Shouldn't it be satisfied—at least for a few days? She heard Israel chuckle beside her. *Damn, I have to remember he can hear what I'm thinking. How does he do that? Fudge puppies, I wonder if Bronx can hear me? Shoot, I'll bet Mr. Stafford can hear me, as well. Geez, this is beyond humbling.*

When Audric Stafford turned to her and grinned, Kenya wished the ground would open up and swallow her whole.

Just shoot me now.

AUDRIC LISTENED AS Lilly West gave a detailed description of the insignia and jewels decorating the knife Denali West took from her assailant. He hoped the young woman kept the damned thing, it would be irrefutable evidence against the group the council had been working years to dismantle. The knife would provide the proof they needed that the group's leader was working actively against the Council and using dark magic for personal and political gain.

The Cardinal Rule in the world of magic was hard and

unchanged since the dawn of time—magical gifts should only be used to make the world a better place. Audric knew as well as anyone, at times, working for the greater good looked self-serving to those who didn't understand the larger picture, but those times were rare and acceptable only when there was no alternative.

There'd been times during Audric's long life when his magical peers believed he was lining his pockets and leveraging his position to gain magical power. Looking back on his youth, he'd made decisions he regretted but tried to make up for those once he'd been in a position to make changes. Audric had never claimed to be perfect. Even now, he felt as though he'd let this problem snowball to this point when it should have been dealt with a hundred years ago.

"Bristol has a similar necklace. When I asked her about it, she told me after the people she knew as her parents died, she found it. Evidently, it was hidden in a small velvet pouch in a box of baby clothes. After everything she's learned, she believes it was hidden by her real mother."

"I'm sure it was." Audric gave Israel a quick nod. "Bristol's parents knew they had been targeted, and it's doubtful they had enough time to make arrangements for their daughter's care. The couple charged with her care were attendants hired by the Council. Unfortunately, it turned out they were more devoted to money than to the child they were hired to protect. When they hadn't been able to find the medallion, they'd taken their frustration out on Bristol."

"It doesn't seem as though the piece was well hidden. If the couple had really been looking for it, wouldn't they have gone through everything? They certainly had enough time." Israel's comment brought nods from many of those around the table, and Audric understood their confusion.

"Remember, you are not dealing with ordinary people. We are talking about highly trained magicals entrusted with a part of one of the most powerful magical tools ever created. The piece was spelled to reveal itself to one person."

Now wasn't the time to ask Bronx if he would be willing to time travel back to the sacred ceremony where the talisman was separated for safekeeping. No one on the Council was present at the ceremony, so there are still many unanswered questions. Audric had been present but hadn't had a clear view. Since the ceremony took place many years before he'd joined the Magic Council, his presence hadn't been noteworthy. One of the biggest challenges they'd faced was confirming how many pieces they were looking for and details of the spell that had been used?

Suddenly noting the awkward silence, Audric chuckled. "Mrs. West, please excuse my distraction. As I'm sure your sons will attest, one of the hazards of leading a team is maintaining your own focus while your mind spins in several directions."

"It was always one of my biggest challenges, and I've seen this look,"—Kyle swept his hand around the circle of men—"more often than I want to admit."

"We may not be able to read minds, but it was always easy to figure out what team members were thinking. Their expressions were always unmistakable. They wanted to know where the hell our minds had gone and an ETA for their return." Kent West's words made Audric smile.

His position as the head of the Magic Council demanded a certain amount of respect, so people were often afraid to speak their minds around him. Usually, the magicals he dealt with watered down their opinions and observations, their comments so bland, conversations were damned boring. Audric had been spending a lot of time in Texas since Charlotte married Austin Adler, and he'd been happy to discover Texans were funny, open-minded, and honest to a fault.

Good thing you enjoy Texas since it looks like you're going to be spending even more time here until we get this mess unraveled.

Auric knew Israel had spoken telepathically in part, to remind him the younger man could hear his thoughts when they were unguarded. He nodded his understanding.

"Before any of you ask, we have people watching every magical we know who is in possession of a piece of the artifact, and I spoke with Catalina before she left—such a remarkable young woman. She was quite helpful and provided us with some missing bits of information pertaining to bringing it back together and the gems mounted on each piece." He took in the looks of interest and knew he was going to have to make a leap of faith, sharing more information than was usually given to anyone outside the council.

"Like any centuries-old establishment, the Magical Council historically operated in secrecy, but this is a problem that has demanded a great deal of cooperation among the members." Audric turned to Lilly, smiling warmly.

"You, my lovely young friend, have given us more information than you know. You've confirmed our suspicions about who we're up against. That information is enormously helpful." Turning to Bronx, Audric said, "I'd like a word with you, but first I'm going to chat with Tobi and her men. I'll be back shortly." Looping Tobi's arm through his, he led the trio to a sheltered area away from the others. Turning to Tobi, he cut straight to the chase. "I understand you lost a baby recently."

"Damn and double damn. I thought Kyle was blunt, but you just might give him some competition."

"Darling, girl. I wanted to talk to you because it's painful to watch people we care about struggle and even more so when they are trying to soldier through the pain in silence." Tobi's face flushed a deep red so quickly, Audric hoped she would forgive him for outing her. He knew his observation was news to her husbands—their expressions had already given them away before he heard their impressive mental run-through of curse words.

"Well, thanks so much for throwing me under the bus. Geez, Louise."

"Kitten, you are already in trouble for keeping this to yourself. I suggest you listen closely to what Audric has to say."

"Yes, sir, of course, you are right." Insincerity practically dripped from Tobi's tone, and Kyle's expression showed he hadn't missed it.

"Tobi, I know you weren't trying to be disrespectful. As much as I'd like to blame my late wife for our youngest daughter's attitude, I'm afraid I will have to shoulder the blame. Brigitte tends to say exactly what's on her mind. It's a trait we share, but I like to consider myself a bit more diplomatic." He gave a negligent shrug, but when her eyes narrowed, he struggled to hold back his laughter. Smart girl—she wasn't buying his nonchalance.

"Mr. Stafford, as much as I appreciate what I'm hoping

is a genuine concern, I'm trying very hard to let the painful memory rest peacefully in my heart."

"Young lady, that was one of the prettiest pieces of... what is it you Texans call it? Horse shit? I never did understand nonmagicals fascination with excrement in their slang, but as the youngsters say, it is what it is." He chuckled when Tobi's mouth dropped open so far, Kent reached over to lift her jaw back in place with his finger.

"Perhaps you could tell us where you were headed with this conversation since I had the impression you were anxious to speak with Bronx?"

Audric nodded, giving Kyle West a reassuring smile.

"I wanted to say I was sorry to hear about your loss. I'm sure you've heard all the platitudes, so I'll save you suffering through any of them again. I wanted to bring you a message from the other side." It was always fun to teach open-minded people how close the link was between magicals and the other side.

"Wait. When you say the other side, are you talking about where our souls go after death?"

"A more accurate description would be, it's where our souls *return* after death. Magicals are in tune with the electrical energy. Every animate and inanimate object has an electrical signature." Shrugging, he flashed them an apologetic smile. "Sorry, I didn't intend for this to become a lecture about how the Universe operates."

"The message?" He could see the hope in Tobi's eyes and was grateful he didn't have to disappoint her.

"Being chosen to host the soul of an angel—even for a short time, is a great honor. Angels need opportunities to learn and grow—I was asked to convey her thanks. She wanted you to know how grateful she is for your help. You see, Tobi, your sadness and feelings of guilt are misplaced because you helped a soul grow in a way no one else could. She wanted you to know she visits often and will never be more than a whispered prayer away."

Watching the change in Tobi's aura was one of the most gratifying things Audric had ever been granted the opportunity to witness. The rusty brown energy field surrounding her dissipated in a fine mist, replaced by a brilliant yellow he felt pulsing with vibrant energy he suspected was the norm before her miscarriage.

When Tobi's eyes filled with tears, Kent and Kyle quickly closed the gap between the three of them, each wrapping an arm around her until she was surrounded. Audric was always in awe when he was given a chance to witness unconditional love because he knew what few others took time to learn—everything in this universe and all others is powered by love.

Satisfied he'd fulfilled his mission, Audric took a step back. Before he could turn away, he saw the grateful looks in Kyle and Kent's eyes. Giving them time alone with Tobi was more important than saying goodbye, so he simply nodded and moved away. His position on the Magic Council usually involved authoritarian decisions in situations where no one was a clear winner. Being able to deliver news, he knew made a positive difference in someone's life, was a blessing. He was thankful the Universe had given him a chance to recharge a bit before requesting a favor from a man he barely knew.

Chapter Nine

"**Y**OU KNOW HE wants you to time travel, right?" Israel's question brought Bronx back to the moment. He'd been lost in thought, wondering how they'd all managed to mate with women linked in such a powerful way.

"I suspected as much, but it's nice to know for sure before he returns." Time travel was a rare magical gift carrying a great deal of responsibility, and Bronx understood how dangerous it could be. Even the smallest action could have enormous repercussions years later. He'd often wondered if whoever wrote the screenplay for the movie, *It's A Wonderful Life,* had experienced time travel because they'd certainly nailed many aspects of it.

Watching Kenya from across the patio, Bronx wasn't surprised to see her attention focused on the lower part of the face of anyone she was talking to. She admitted it was much more difficult for her to hear women, so he was grateful Lilly and Gracie were making sure they included her in their conversation.

Kenya looked up, her gaze scanning the room until she found him. Bronx was pleased to see her body relax once she knew he was close. He held out his hand to her and smiled at the pink blush staining her cheeks as she moved to him. Tucking her close to his side, Bronx watched Audric approach, the tension in his shoulders easy to see.

"Bronx, let's move further into the shade. I'm afraid I don't always remember how warm it is here in the afternoon."

Kenya smiled at the older man as they walked closer to the building.

"The heat was a huge adjustment for me when I first moved to Texas. We moved a lot when I was a kid, but my mom seemed to avoid the south for some reason."

"Over the course of my exceptionally long life, I've learned people rarely do things without reason. The key is uncovering the hidden as well as the obvious answers." Audric's words were as true as any Bronx had ever heard. Being able to dial into a person's motivation was one of the things he learned early in his business career. Now he wondered how much different it would be to look back on what had driven Kenya's mother to make what looked like a litany of bad choices.

"I know I should be more interested in why she did certain things, but to be honest, it took me a long time to get past that stage, and I'm not sure I want to go back. There doesn't seem to be a lot to be gained from rehashing all those painful memories."

Bronx hated the sadness he felt surround his mate. He was grateful for the distraction when Gracie set down a tray filled with ice-cold glasses of lemonade as Lilly approached with another tray filled with sandwiches and cookies.

"You ladies will spoil me, and my daughters will make

a lot of noise about how I shouldn't get used to being treated like royalty."

Bronx laughed as the man flirted shamelessly with every woman he encountered—maybe getting older had a few advantages after all since no one seemed to take offense. To their credit, Gracie and Lilly didn't linger. After they'd made certain everyone was comfortable and promising to check back later, they'd moved back to the pool area.

"I'm not going to waste your time with a lot of small talk, Bronx. The Council tasked me with asking you to time travel back to the ceremony where the magical artifact was divided. Since none of the members of the council were there and we have no written record, we need as much information as we can get to figure out what we're up against."

"What makes you believe you're up against anything?" Bronx was grateful for Israel's insight and support. He wasn't afraid to ask Audric the hard questions many people would shy away from because of the man's position of power in the magical community.

"When all five male members of one magical family are mated with women who have pieces of a powerful magical artifact—something is up. You and I both know there is no such thing as coincidence, Israel."

"I understand why it looks odd, but I sought Bronx out. My mom didn't give me any specific information, other than telling me when I found the other half, and the magic would be enough to fix my hearing and make certain I had a place to live. It took me months of reading those blasted books to figure out where I needed to go."

"Those books were stolen recently, correct?" Kenya's

hesitant nod was her only response to Audric's question. "Whoever took the books obviously believes they contain more than the location of another piece of the artifact." Bronx agreed. It would have been easy enough for the thief to simply follow Kenya and take the amulets once she'd located the other half. Whoever took the journals was looking for more than one piece.

"Do you think I'll ever get them back?" Kenya's voice cracked with emotion as she asked the question.

Bronx suspected she already knew the answer—there wasn't a chance in hell those books would be recovered, and his heart ached for her. It had to have been devastating to lose something she obviously treasured. He and his siblings cherished the few personal mementos they'd each kept from their parents' home—knowing something she loved had been taken from her made Bronx want to hurt those responsible.

"I don't believe that's likely, Kenya, and I know it's disappointing. What I can offer is to recreate them from your memory if you're willing to allow me inside." Bronx wasn't sure who was more surprised by the offer—hell, he hadn't even known it was possible.

"You can do that? How is it possible?" Kenya waved her hand around in a circle before sighing. "Pickled pigs tails, why am I questioning a man I'm sure is as high ranking as any magical I'll ever meet? Good grief, sometimes the things that come out of my mouth embarrass me to pieces." Audric smiled warmly as Bronx and Israel both chuckled softly.

"You're going to have to step up the embarrassing comments several notches to even be noticed in our family, Kenya." Israel's reassurance was not only welcome, it was also accurate. Almost every one of them had gone through phases where they spoke first and put their brains in gear later. Asia was the only one who always seemed to be in control—she was called the Adler Ice Princess for good reason.

"It is a very complicated spell, and you are right to assume it isn't something an inexperienced witch or wizard would be able to do." Audric leaned forward, taking Kenya's hand, holding it between his own. The differences between them startling, and the picture was one Bronx knew he'd never forget. It was a lesson in life—youth at one end of the spectrum, juxtaposed against age and wisdom at the other. "Did you read the journals in any particular order?"

"I read them in reverse date order, incorrectly assuming my mother wouldn't have written down anything important until after she'd given me the amulet. As it turned out, all the details of her friendship with Mrs. Adler were in the earliest volumes, including their promises to each other to give their halves to their children."

"I know you're feeling a small measure of betrayal because it looks as though you were misled about the number of pieces, but that isn't the case. Remember, these are pieces of history. They've been passed down for generations—generations of magicals who lived long lives. The original magical totem was divided to protect and preserve its power. Without an official from the Council present, they were able to skirt any requirements for written documentation. I was there, but I wasn't able to see everything." Audric took a deep breath and turned his attention to Bronx.

"There are only a handful of magicals who have your particular skill set, and you are the only one with a mate who can camouflage to hide our presence." Every muscle in Bronx's body tightened when Audric suggested Kenya accompany him while time traveling. What the hell was the man thinking? The elderly wizard held up his hand when Bronx opened his mouth to argue. "I know it's dangerous, and I wouldn't ask if I had any other option. I will be tagging along to provide an additional layer of security."

"I would also like to go along, but I'm not sure it's wise." Bronx sensed Israel's inner struggle as he tried to balance his need to protect his brother and fear of leaving his own mate's security in someone else's hands.

"No, it will be important for every member of your family to stay close to their mates." Bronx understood what Audric hadn't bothered to explain—mates could protect one another better than anyone else could. "I'm not discounting the safety concerns you have for Kenya, quite the opposite actually. Having her with you serves multiple purposes."

"Excuse me, could you please stop talking about me as if I wasn't here? I've been making my own decisions for a long time, and I'm perfectly capable of making this one." Bronx looked at the other two men and saw the same apology and respect he felt was also shining in their eyes. "The way I see it, there are several issues with Mr. Stafford's plan, but the most significant is that Bronx and I haven't... well, we haven't nailed down all the details of this mating thing."

Nailed down?

Damn, brother—you're slacking in your old age.

Fuck you. Hell, now he was waging a telepathic battle of junior high level wits with his younger brother like they were kids instead of grown men. Bronx nearly groaned out loud when he glanced over to see Audric Stafford fight back his smile. No magical wanted to look immature in front of the most powerful wizard in the world—and it was even more humbling since his granddaughter was now a part of their family.

Before Bronx could assure Audric he and his mate would be having a meaningful discussion about mating, the wizard pulled a phone from his pocket and excused himself to take a call. Reaching into his pocket, Bronx pressed the button on the small remote and smiled when Kenya let out a small squeak. No doubt she'd forgotten about the tiny bullet vibrator nestled deep in her core. Activating it now was more a statement than play. Bronx wanted her to remember who she belonged to—at this point, claiming her was more of a formality than anything else.

"I'll leave the two of you to work this out. Bristol will be ready to leave the hospital soon, and I want to be there to escort her home." Pulling Kenya into a quick hug before setting her back and grinning down at her. "Behave, or you're going to find yourself draped over Bronx's knees, and I'm sure he'd much rather introduce you to the joys of erotic spanking rather than a punishment paddling." Bronx watched Kenya's eyes widen before her cheeks flamed with embarrassment.

Once they were alone, Bronx sat down on one of the padded chairs before pulling her onto his lap. Turning

Kenya so he could see her face, Bronx wrapped his hand around her wrist, smoothing the pad of his thumb over her pulse until their heartbeats synchronized.

"How do you do that?" He wasn't going to insult her intelligence by pretending he didn't understand the question.

"We are fated mates, *Chef*. The Universe takes care of its own, and a large part of that is making certain we're compatible. The synchronization of our heartbeats is a significant part of the mating process and confirms what I knew from the moment your scent surrounded me. It's calming—giving both us a sense of peace when we're close. The deep comfort we both feel when our hearts beat as one is important for bonding. In the future, we'll be in synch even when we're apart. If the synchronization is disrupted, the other mate will recognize it immediately. Consider it a sort of built-in alarm system." As a blood born shifter, he'd be able to track his mate anywhere in the world by scent alone.

I don't deserve this. I was going to steal something his mother gave him for stars' sake. If I stall, he'll come to his senses and bolt... taking the damned amulet with him, and it's no more than I deserve.

Loneliness and despair surrounded him, the thick waves of emotion, making Bronx feel like he was being sucked into a dark vortex. He didn't need to ask Kenya where she'd gotten the mistaken impression, she wasn't worthy of being loved. There'd been hints in everything she'd said about her mother.

"There are some things you need to know about mates. I've mentioned some of them, but those points bear repeating. Fate never makes a mistake, and we've been mated for a reason. Mates are attracted to each other physically, even if they aren't like anyone you've ever been attracted to in the past. Some shifters wait decades to find their mates, and fate always finds a way to ensure their paths cross."

"Letting someone bite me is damned scary."

Bronx appreciated her honesty and was more than a little relieved to find out this was her biggest concern because he'd make certain she was so distracted, it didn't occur to her to be scared.

"I promise to make this one of the most spectacular experiences of your life. I want it to be a sweet memory you carry with you forever. This is on me, I've let you worry about this far too long. Let's go." He should have claimed her in the shower when he first took her home.

Tell Audric we'll be ready to travel tomorrow. The two of you work out the details and text me.

Already set up—you're predictable, big brother.

As much as Bronx loved his brothers and sisters, there were times when they were a real pain in the ass.

KENYA APPEARED TO be lost in thought as Bronx drove through the gates and down the long drive toward his house. He only lived a few minutes from the club, but they'd been stopped so many times before they could make their escape, the trip seemed much longer than it actually was.

"What's more frightening, being mated or traveling

back in time?" When she didn't answer right away, Bronx wondered if she was considering the two options he'd given her or if there was something else on her mind. The word *deserve* floated through his mind again as he parked in the garage. When he placed his hand over hers, Kenya seemed startled to realize he'd already turned off the engine.

"Talk to me, Kenya. We are mates. No one in the entire world will ever care more about your hopes, dreams, and fears than I do. I want to be the first person you think about sharing good news with as well as the one you run to when you need a shoulder to cry on." The garage lights were slowly dimming, but he didn't miss the single tear trailing down her perfect cheek, its silvery trail glistening in the fading light.

"I'm afraid to be happy."

Was she serious? The answer seemed so odd, at first, he wanted to outright discount it—but he'd learned people rarely lie when they are admitting a personal failing, which meant she'd probably reveal something deeper if he was willing to listen. The moment would be lost if he moved her into the house, so he stayed still and waited. "It's probably more accurate to say, I'm afraid to let down my guard and enjoy the moment. Every time I've let myself relax, I've been blindsided."

"Give me an example, so I'm sure I understand what you're saying."

"The apartment I was living in was perfect. It was cheap, close to the campus where I was taking a class, and also close to the small coffee shop where I found a part-time job." She took a deep breath and seemed to sink deeper into the supple leather seat. "It was also close to the dealership where I knew you spent most of your time. I needed to be able to watch you, learn your habits." She finally met his gaze, regret easy to see, but it was the start pain of loneliness that made his heart clench.

"Guilt erodes the soul, *Cher*. If I'm not holding it against you, I don't think you should either. Your mother convinced you the other half of a totem held the answers to your prayers—all you had to do was find it. Let me ask you this—why did you stall for so long? What changed?" He knew her soul had recognized him as her mate. What he needed was for her to see it for herself.

"My landlord wanted to... *barter* my rent. When I refused, he evicted me to give the place to a woman he was already seeing on the side." Bronx suspected her previous address was in the report Israel put together—he'd make certain the man paid for what he'd done to Kenya. "Before you point out that he can't legally evict me if I was paying rent, save it. We all know how easy it is to get around those rules." She was right, there were enough loopholes in most rental agreements for an elephant to waltz through.

"You're stalling, mate. Tell me what made you put off trying to steal my amulet."

"I liked you." The words came out in a rush, and he knew the hurried admission surprised her. "I saw how nice you were to people, and as crazy as it seems, I could tell you suspected someone was breaking in. I could feel your awareness. Why didn't you call the police?"

Aww, his mate was no one's fool. Good.

"There was something about the residual ripples of

103

your energy—something in those lingering vibrations I recognized. I knew we hadn't met, but there was something... something I couldn't identify." He'd suspected the little intruder was his mate, but until he'd scented her in the alley, there wasn't a way to be sure. She watched him for long seconds before giving him a small smile.

"Touché."

Chapter Ten

I'M GOING TO *burst into flames if he doesn't get on with it.* She and Bronx shared a shower, which gave new meaning to the word steamy, before tumbling into his enormous bed. He moved to the foot of the bed, grasped her ankles, and spread her legs wide. Staring at her exposed pussy, Bronx didn't make any attempt to hide his appreciation.

"Fucking beautiful. I love looking at your pretty pink pussy lips. Seeing them flowering open as blood rushes into the tender tissues makes it easy to see why the ancients compared a woman's sex to a rose." He trailed the tips of his fingers through her wet labia, and Kenya felt another rush of her slick arousal pulse from her core. Her cheeks flushed with heat, and she knew her face was glowing bright enough to light the room—not that she'd know since she'd closed her eyes and groaned in embarrassment.

"Don't hide from me, mate. I want to look into your eyes while I play with you. Don't be embarrassed by your body's reaction to me. Hell, your sweet cream is the hottest thing I've ever seen. I'm thrilled you respond so perfectly to my touch. Your body recognizes your mate even if your head is still trying to make sense of it all."

Goddess in heaven, Kenya wanted him to take her. She

knew patience was the name of the game in foreplay, but suddenly it seemed to her, the concept was vastly overrated.

"Are you going to wax poetic all night about my pussy or fuck me?" Holy shit! Had she really said that out loud? She watched his brows raise as surprise moved over his face. Hell, astonishment was a better description. Before she could apologize, he threw his head back and laughed.

"I don't ever want to compare you to any other woman because you are unique in so many ways. You are my mate, the only woman I'll be intimate with from this point forward, but I have to say, I don't ever remember a woman making me laugh while we were in bed. Ordinarily, your outburst would earn you at least ten, *Chef*, but we need to have a chat about safe words and limits first. Tonight is different. I want you as much as you seem to want to be taken. I assure you I'll give you everything you need, but we're going at my pace."

Kenya felt the deep blush of embarrassment fading and hoped he realized how much she wanted him. She wondered what was most attractive—the way he spoke to her, his heavy-lidded look of desire, or his model good looks. Everything about the man was hot.

Leaning forward, Bronx used the rolled tip of his tongue to lick the wet folds of her sex and groaned. "Your taste ignites a fire in my soul, my lovely mate. I want to spend hours lapping up every sweet drop of your honey. I'd love nothing more than to spend days on end, sending you sailing into the blissful oblivion of sexual release, your mind so fractured by the pleasure, you'll forget your own name." Tracing the engorged petals of her pussy, Bronx placed his large hands atop her thighs, holding her in place when tried to arch off the bed in response to his touch.

"Stay still, or I'll tie you to the bed." Kenya's body responded before her mind could process whether the words were a threat or promise. Why did the thought of being tied down, unable to do anything but endure every erotic pleasure he was willing to give her, make Kenya's body feel like it was catching fire? The man was lethal, and by some twist of fate, he was hers.

"Yes, *Cheŕ*, I belong to you, just as you belong to me. Now, let's see if I can still that busy mind of yours."

There wasn't time for her mind to question how he'd known what she'd been thinking before Bronx sent her spiraling into a vortex of pleasure where nothing existed outside the heat of her body's response. Color burst all around her, and Kenya heard a woman scream. It took several seconds for her to become cognizant enough to notice he'd turned her over and was helping her to her hands and knees.

When the flaming heat of Bronx's chest pressed against her back, Kenya's arms threatened to fold out from under her. He slid his muscled arm around her, securing her smaller body against his much larger one. The sensation was as comforting as it was arousing. Goddess above, Kenya was turning into a damned poetic sap, and she couldn't find the strength to care. All she cared about was getting him inside her. Instinct trumped reason, and Kenya felt her body ready itself for his possession.

"You're testing me, mate. Stretching my control past

any reasonable expectation." His hand slid slowly over her flat stomach until the tips of his fingers skimmed her clit. "Perfect, your pretty little pearl has come out to play, baby. We'll do slow and easy next time. I want you too much to do anything but fast and hard this round." She felt the blazing tip of his cock teasing her entrance and tried to thrust back to force his possession, but he wasn't having it. "No, *Cher*. Stay still. You are so tight. Hell, I'm not even inside, and I can feel you closing around the tip of my cock. I don't want to bruise or tear any of those tender tissues."

"Please, I'm going to die if you don't get inside." She could hear the desperation in her voice, and it wasn't surprising since that's exactly what she felt. In a flash of insight, Kenya saw a paw, a huge black paw clawing at what appeared to be a thin shell. The animal was larger than any dog she'd ever seen if its wide foot was anything to go by. Every cell in her body felt electrified as her body thundered toward release, and the animal she finally recognized as a wolf became clearer in her mind's eye.

"You are so much more than I deserve and miles above what I dared to hope for, *Cher*." He used one arm to hold himself over her, his hips pressing slowly, pushing the thick shaft of his cock forward. *Slowly*, that was the damned keyword. She was going insane, waiting for him to take her, claim her, set the animal inside him free.

Gasping at the sudden realization there was a wolf inside her as well turned her world upside down. She could see the lighter colored paws clawing to be set free but instinctively knew she wasn't ready for that yet. How had she not known? Her body was trembling, bombarded by sensations so intense, Kenya wondered if she'd survive. Bronx's warm breath wafted over her shoulder, and his chest was so tight against her back, she could feel his heartbeat pounding against her spine.

Bronx withdrew from her heat, leaving the rippling muscles lining her vagina clenching at the sudden emptiness she felt all the way to her soul. He'd withdrawn until only the head of his cock remained inside, and the anticipation of the first hard thrust was almost more than she could bear. She felt his tongue glide along the top of her shoulder, lapping at the tender spot where it sloped up—close enough to her neck, Kenya knew he could feel her pulse thundering just beneath the skin.

"Tell me you want to be mine, Kenya. Tell me to claim you, to set the wolf inside you free." She should have known he'd have seen her animal just as she had. There would never be any secrets between them.

"Please. Yes. Yours." Three words gasped in a voice fractured by a need so intense, it defied description, but it was enough.

His hips thrust forward with enough force, his balls bounced against her clit, and the combination launched her over the edge. Lights exploded behind her eyelids as she tumbled headfirst into a swirling tornado of color. Somewhere in the back of her mind, Kenya felt a stinging bite a split second before her blood felt as if it was boiling in her veins, every nerve ending in her body vibrating. The residual power from the blast of electricity following his bite was disconcerting.

Her entire being felt as though it was being tossed end over end, floundering in a turbulent sea of sexual pleasure greater than anything she'd ever imagine possible. Blinking, Kenya was shocked to realize she was on her side. Bronx laid curled around her, his arm holding her against his chest. When he spoke, his voice was so loud in her ear, Kenya gasped. His fingers gently pulled her hearing aids from her ears.

"Sorry, *Cher*, I forgot to warn you, you won't need these anymore. You'll find all of your senses are greatly enhanced now that we've mated and your inner wolf brought out of hiding. It will be a while before you are ready to shift, so don't force it."

BRONX WAS LEVELED. His muscles trembled from exertion and the sudden influx of his mate's DNA coursing through his system. The physical changes wouldn't be as great for him since he'd already been shifting for years. It shocked him to learn Kenya had an inner wolf. He knew when she'd seen his, then he'd seen the same vision of hers just a few seconds before his fangs punctured the tender skin at the junction of her neck and shoulder.

The fresh scent of her warm, moist skin had been too much to resist. Damn, he was glad she'd agreed to be his because he wasn't sure he would have been able to resist. Now he understood how Austin lost control and claimed Charlotte before she'd agreed to belong to him. He'd thought he was prepared for the intensity of mating, but it was so much more than he'd anticipated.

The heat the two of them generated was like the flash

fires his dealerships occasionally experienced in their mechanic shops when torches were used too close to flammable liquids. He'd have sworn his blood was nearing the boiling point before the sensation finally began to subside. Nothing had prepared him for what he'd experienced.

"I died, didn't I? I did. I know I did, and you're just afraid to tell me. It should probably worry me since no angels have shown up to escort me to the pearly gates. Do shifters go to heaven? Maybe I should be hiding under the bed just in case someone from the other team shows up. Damn, it's going to really suck if I don't get to enjoy not wearing hearing aids any longer than this."

Bronx chuckled but didn't have the energy to move so he could look at her.

"Lie still for a few minutes and let all those lovely little molecules roll around in the DNA mix we've created. I'm told it takes a few minutes to bounce back, but then we'll have energy to spare." His brothers all swore it was true, but Bronx was starting to think this might be another of the pranks they loved playing on each other. Hell, it had been like this since they were kids—several of them concocted a story and proceeded to gaslight one of their brothers or sisters. They'd learned early on, it was useless to try to fool Austin or Asia, but the rest of the group had been fair game—more than once.

"Your family sounds like fun. I can't imagine what it had to be like having that many people who loved you."

"Or that many kids in one house. Hell, most of the time, it was what our parents affectionately referred to as organized chaos." He'd finally recovered enough to turn her, so he could look at the woman who'd turned his entire world on end. Using the pads of his fingers, Bronx brushed the wayward strands of her hair away from her face.

The glow of the bedside lamp cast a soft golden light over her bare skin, the dim rays painting a picture with shadows and light Bronx made certain he committed to memory. As an amateur photographer, he could hardly wait to take pictures of Kenya. He'd do his best to recreate the vision in front of him but knew there was no way it would ever be as perfect as this moment.

"Only if you promise no one will ever see the pictures. And just so you know, I'm not particularly photogenic."

"I'm going to enjoy proving you wrong, *Chef*. The camera tells the truth as the photographer sees it. People who don't believe the camera treats them fairly haven't found the right artist... one who uses his camera to paint the picture—that makes all the difference." They were lost in their own thoughts for a few minutes, letting the silence settle around them like a soft blanket on a chilly winter night. He was grateful she didn't feel the need to fill the stillness surrounding them.

"Silence? You must be kidding. I'm enjoying the symphony of sound. The wind is whispering names as it skims past the windows. Refusing to be excluded, there are baby birds in the nest outside the sliding glass doors, calling to their mother, impatient at being kept waiting for their dinner. So many small mouths to feed, she flies to and fro in a frantic race to silence their pleading before the next round begins in the morning. The waves at the lake are lapping at the shore, the beat increasing as the moon moves across the night sky. I can hardly wait to visit the ocean and listen to the tide roll in and out."

Bronx was dumbfounded. It was damned humbling to realize how much he took for granted. She looked at him, eyes wide with wonder as she added, "I'm never going to forget this moment. I haven't been able to hear the ticking of a clock or birds sing since I was very young."

"It might be overwhelming for a while. I've spoken to people who got hearing aids and were unpleasantly surprised by how difficult it was to adapt to the noisy world around them." More than one of his employees who'd taken advantage of the company's willingness to help them purchase hearing aids reported the adjustment was much more difficult than they anticipated. He saw a tear break free from the corner of her eye to flow quickly over her temple, disappearing in the silky strands of her sex-tousled hair. Before he could ask, she shook her head, and the stark look of appreciation and reverence in her eyes surprised him.

"I'll be able to hear children playing in the park. One of the worst parts of losing my hearing was not being able to hear their lighthearted laughter as they hung upside down from the monkey bars and slid down the slipper-slides. I used to love hearing the kids on the playground laugh as they finally mastered how to swing higher and higher until they felt like they could touch the sky."

"I feel like an ungrateful fool, *Chef*. I've been able to do all those things and not once thanked the Universe for the privilege."

"It's easy to forget how lucky we are. I didn't have

many creature comforts or the security of a large, loving family, but I should have been more grateful for what I had. I know my mom would have enjoyed her life more without the burden of a child, but she kept me with her, anyway. So many times, I have wished I'd taken time to say thank you." She paused for a minute before sighing. "There were a few times when she'd been drinking and let down her guard. Those were the rare moments when she spoke about my father and how she hoped she could hide me forever. I've often wondered if she'd been worried about our safety or simply angry at him for leaving."

Bronx felt the hair on the back of his neck stand on end—a sure sign Kenya's words held some sort of significance. He wasn't sure what it meant, but he knew something important was on the horizon. Following his gut had always served him well, and Bronx wouldn't ignore what he considered a head's up from the Universe. Nature was a force more powerful than anything mankind or magicals could match, and it liked to remind souls how important it was to listen to the whispered warnings.

Chapter Eleven

B RONX LEANED BACK in the padded chair, elbows resting on the armrests, his fingers steepled in front of his face as he watched Kenya walk along the edge of the lake. She retraced the same steps time and again, making him smile as she took in everything around her. He'd listened in on her thoughts until Audric Stafford arrived a few minutes ago. Listening to the remarkable way her mind worked fascinated him.

"She's quite gifted, you know. I'm surprised Lisa was able to keep it hidden." Bronx didn't respond, knowing it was best to let the man tell the story in his own time. "Lisa wasn't a powerful witch, and what little she learned before striking out on her own, she owed to your mother. It's true the two of them became friends, but that wasn't the way it started. Your mother was assigned to mentor Lisa—to help her control her magic and channel it appropriately. Damn, that girl was as wild as the wind."

"I assume she was a rogue since Kenya hasn't mentioned any other family."

"Yes, no one in their family had ever been blessed with magic until Lisa. They had no idea what to do with her and kicked her out of their home when she was sixteen. She came to the attention of the Council when she tried to use magic to steal food. Long story short, she was doing well until a young man from a prominent magical family in Europe decided she was fair game. When she turned up pregnant, his family announced they would take care of Lisa until the baby was born, pay her off, and she would never see her child again."

Bronx slid his sunglasses down his tanned nose and arched a brow. He wasn't surprised—wealthy magical families didn't always play by the rules, and those with old European money were among the worst. Ruthless was the word most often used to describe them.

"Lisa was often a mess of the first order, but she wasn't stupid. She didn't believe the Fitzpatricks would hold up their end of the bargain Lisa was convinced she would hand over the child and be dead before the next sunrise—so she ran. She'd learned enough from Brighten to hide until her drug addiction stole the self-control she needed to maintain the shield. The Council was watching, or at least we felt like we were, but it's obvious we failed miserably in many ways."

And Kenya paid the price.

Bronx didn't know what to say. Actually, there was a lot he wanted to say, but nothing remotely respectful, and there was nothing to be gained by losing an ally.

Audric smiled, "You couldn't say anything I haven't said to myself a thousand times. I could have taken Kenya from Lisa at any time. Hell, I traced her magical signature more than once. It was important to know Kenya was safe and to warn Lisa about what the Council considered questionable parenting."

Bronx could see regret reflected in Stafford's eyes and wondered how often the man looked back on difficult decisions, second-guessing his choices.

"After your parents died, all hell broke loose. The Council knew we were teetering on the edge of a magical war unlike anything any of us had ever dealt with, and to be honest, I was up to my ass in alligators, as you southerners are fond of saying. I was distracted and thought I was too damned busy to keep track of one young witch and her child." Audric set aside the cup of coffee he'd brought with him. Bronx shook his head as the ceramic mug slowly faded from view.

"She isn't going to stay out there much longer. Why don't you tell me what you're holding back, so we can work it out before she joins us? Kenya is going to have enough to deal with, so I'd like to shield her from as many problems as possible."

"The amulet Lisa gave to Kenya wasn't passed down to her by family. Lisa stole it from Sean Fitzpatrick when she learned she was pregnant with his child, and he made it clear he wasn't ready for a family. I have little doubt there will be a member of the Fitzpatrick family at the division ceremony. Kenya bears a striking resemblance to her great-grandmother, so it is important to keep her out of sight if it's at all possible." There was something amiss with what Audric was telling him—not exactly a lie, but the lines around the truth were certainly being blurred.

"She has every right to have the amulet since it belonged to her father. I realize it was an ill-gotten gain, but I'm assuming her father is deceased since you referred to him in the past tense."

"Yes, he was killed in an accident eerily similar to the one that claimed your parents. I believe the accidents are related to the amulets, but at this time, we don't have any way to prove it." Bronx shifted his attention from Audric to where Kenya stood watching them. She was still at the water's edge, but it was easy to see her attention was focused on the two men sitting on the terrace. "She's no fool, Bronx, and she's far more gifted than her mother. Kenya will take all the pieces she's picking up from this conversation and fit them together faster than any of us can anticipate."

"When do you plan to tap into her memory to recreate the journals? I'm looking forward to seeing how the process works. Hell, I didn't even know it was possible." Bronx knew there were vast areas of the world of magic he had never been exposed to, and he was looking forward to learning more.

"I've already been pulling bits and pieces of the journals from her memory. Recreating the journals is the easy part. I've never been comfortable poking around in someone's memories. I may not have grown up with the importance of privacy protections drilled into me the way you Americans do, but I've always understood the implications of exposing secrets the other person had no intention of sharing. The rest of my inquiry could trigger deeply buried memories. I have asked for another gifted magicals help because another woman might anticipate the landmines. She's going to need your support when she realizes the enormity of her family connections."

Bronx shook his head as he considered how much deeper this mess was going to get before he and his mate were free to enjoy each other's company. Damn it all to hell. He'd worked hard his entire life, looking forward to the time he found his mate and started his own family. His father spent a tremendous amount of time with his wife and children, never favoring business over family. Of course, Carrington Adler's business had been teetering on the brink of collapse when he died—his financial demise in large part due to the time he spent at home rather than taking care of the oil company he'd founded.

There had been many times when Bronx wondered if perhaps his father had somehow known his time on this side of the veil was coming to an end. That knowledge would have driven him to spend as much time with his family as possible. Carrington Adler left a business on the cusp of failure, but the life lessons his children learned during their family's travels and late-night chats sitting at the kitchen bar were like stones thrown in a still pond. The ripples from his mom and dad's guidance and ever-patient wisdom overlapped, building one on another, reaching places no one could have ever anticipated.

Bronx knew his business would thrive without him micromanaging the dealerships. He'd worked hard to have everything in place when his mate finally made her appearance. He didn't want to ever be in a position where he had to make a choice between making certain his wife and children knew how much they meant to him and risking their financial future. Thanks to Austin's business acumen, all the Adler siblings had trust funds, ensuring they could live comfortably without ever working another day. The last Bronx knew, none of them had touched their accounts for anything other than furthering their education or investing in their respective businesses.

Kenya walked toward them, drawing his undivided attention. She was beauty and grace personified—it was part of what mesmerized him when he'd watched her in the security feeds. The way she moved reminded him of his sister, Brooklyn. Even as a kid, Brooklyn had been able to sneak up on anyone, including Israel, whose telepathic abilities usually ensured he was acutely aware of anyone nearby. Kenya's ability to camouflage herself reminded him of Brooklyn, eluding the most sophisticated security systems in the world. By the time she retired, B had retrieved over a billion dollars in stolen goods.

"Being compared to your sister is a mixed blessing." Kenya's teasing tone pulled Bronx back to the moment. Shaking his head to dislodge the fog of distraction plaguing him this morning, Bronx tried to calm his frustration.

"The fog will clear in a few hours." Audric's reassurance was a relief—damn, it was frustrating to have his mind wandering around like an unattended preschooler. "Some shifters experience an increase in their sexual appetite so acute, it's uncontrollable. I'd say you are functioning rather well, all things considered. At least your pack hasn't dropped a net over the two of you and locked you in your wing of their home."

Bronx knew Audric was trying to lighten the mood, but it didn't appear Kenya was in the mood to be distracted.

"Do you have time to answer some questions, Mr. Stafford?"

"Certainly, but I would prefer you called me Audric—it seems only fitting if I'm going to act as your substitute grandfather." Bronx chuckled when the older man winked at Kenya. It was impossible to be angry when it obvious Audric had a soft spot for Kenya.

As her mate, it was his job to ensure her safety and provide her with everything she needed to feel satisfied. In his view, making sure she understood everything they were facing fell under that umbrella.

"I know you're a busy man, and I don't want to keep you from any pressing... umm, well, what is it do you do exactly?" Kenya's cheeks flushed with embarrassment as Audric leaned back and laughed.

"Dear, that's a million-dollar question, and one not easily answered. As the head of the Magic Council, I share many duties with the other members, but the one that seems to take up most of my time is censuring magicals who have overstepped their boundaries in one way or another."

"Is there some kind of chain of command? A lower court? I'm sorry if my questions seem childish, but my mother always became belligerent if I asked any questions about the magical world."

"Your mother was envious of your gifts, Kenya. She knew your magic was much more powerful than her own. She wanted to keep you hidden for as long as possible." Audric studied her closely, and Bronx could practically hear the man's thoughts assessing how much to share... how much she was ready to hear.

"There were a few times when she was drinking or experiencing one of her manic swings, she'd rave on and on, saying my father's family would kidnap and torture me if they were given a chance. She would never tell me any more about them, so the only way I could make sure I didn't give myself away to them was to keep myself as isolated as possible."

"Kenya, your mother had a lot of personal issues unrelated to you. She'd stolen a powerful piece of magical history, and most people felt she wasn't responsible enough to be entrusted with something so significant. Her ancestors weren't one of the families originally given one of the pieces to guard—your father's family was."

They are going to take it from me. Better to cut and run now.

The unspoken words barely registered in Bronx mind before the unmistakable scent of fear surrounded him. The realization Kenya believed anyone would take what was rightfully hers made his heart ache. Shifters were known for their keen awareness, something he was grateful for now. Between one breath and the next, he saw her pulse pounding at the base of her neck, kicking up several notches as her muscles tensed. Before he could reach for her, Kenya's fight-or-flight response flipped, and she turned to run. With a simple wave of his hand, Audric froze her in place.

"Kenya, I hate using magic to force you to listen, but panic always trumps logic, so this was the only way I could make certain you heard me out."

Bronx moved to stand in front of his newly claimed mate, brushing the backs of his fingers over her cheek and pressing a kiss against her sweat-soaked forehead. Her eyes were pleading for his help, but as much as he hated seeing her unhappy, Audric was right. Pure panic had fueled her reaction. There was another trace scent so subtle, he would have missed it if he hadn't been looking in her eyes and seen the flash of sadness.

Kenya's breathing was becoming shallow and much too fast. Bronx didn't want Audric to use a spell to calm her—it would work, but it wouldn't help build the bond of trust they needed for the challenges he knew they would face traveling back in time. It was important for Kenya to learn she could put herself fully in his hands. She'd need to respond to commands without hesitation to ensure her safety during their trip. Audric's magic was powerful, but it wouldn't be enough to pull her back to the present if anything went wrong. The magical skill required for time travel was specific and rare—it was also dangerous.

"*Cher*, look at me. Listen to my voice. Concentrate on what I'm telling you." It took her a few seconds to lock her gaze to his and another moment before Bronx knew he had her undivided attention. "No one will take what's yours. Audric will release you as soon as your panic fades. Don't listen to your fear, mate." He could hear her mind rolling his words over as she tried to pull herself back from the edge. Damn, he was proud of her.

In his peripheral vision, Bronx saw Audric wave his hand. Tiny pinpricks of light flew from his fingertips floating through the air to encircle Kenya. Bronx was grateful he already had his hands on her because the subtle release of the spell made Kenya drop like a marionette whose strings had been cut.

"Okay, Audric, we need to have a chat." Kenya's words were airy and fainter than usual, but despite her lack of physical strength, Bronx could hear a thread of newfound respect for magic. "Just because you can do something doesn't always mean you should. I'm a reasonable person... well, most of the time... usually. You could have just yelled like a normal person." Audric laughed and shook his head.

"I swear, your mother was a hot mess. We warned her too many times about her explosive temper and poor parenting. Yelling is not what normal people do, Kenya."

"I'm not sure normal people freeze people in their tracks by shooting electric currents out the end of their fingers either, but we'll save that discussion for another time." Bronx eased his mate onto his lap, relieved when she relaxed against him. "If you were a doctor, people would question your bedside manner. You might want to read that book about winning friends and influencing people. I can't remember who wrote it—some librarian."

"Dale Carnegie wrote the book. He wasn't a librarian but was a prolific writer and renowned lecturer. Andrew Carnegie was the industrialist whose name adorns many prestigious libraries and other buildings. They weren't related but were both interesting men." Audric's blasé attitude when speaking of historical figures was almost amusing. Bronx had always wished his gift would allow him to spend time with the men and women who'd shaped the world, but those conversations might well influence thinking and therefore, change decisions. History wasn't his to alter, something his parents stressed repeatedly.

Chapter Twelve

S TANDING UNDER THE gently cascading water of Bronx's outdoor shower, Kenya stretched her arms above her head and leaned side to side, hoping to loosen some of the tension she'd been feeling since her conversation with Audric Stafford. Bronx was right, there was something about showering outside that set her spirit free. It was humbling to learn so much of what she'd been told was a half-truth at best. Hell, a lot of it was patently false.

Hearing her mother had stolen the medallion from her father and his family made her question everything her mom had ever told her. One of the hard lessons Kenya learned growing up was lying was a slippery slope—the first led to a second and a third. Lies were like cockroach-es—if you discovered one, there were a hundred more lurking behind the walls.

"I don't even want to know how you've gone from enjoying the freedom of being naked outside to thinking about cockroaches." Kenya squeaked in surprise when her mate's words wafted over the shell of her ear. When she tried to turn, her feet slipped on the wet tile, but he kept her from falling, wrapping his arms around her. Kenya felt her body respond to his naked warmth pressed against her back. "You spend too much time thinking and not enough time feeling, mate."

Bronx knew his siblings would be the first to call him out for his hypocrisy. He'd been so focused on his career, he'd missed more than one family function. It wasn't easy to admit, but he'd heard the same comment from several of the women he'd dated over the years. None of them were willing to be relegated to a distant second in his life, and he hadn't blamed them.

"I was thinking about all the lies my mom told me. Why didn't she tell me the truth? At the very least, she should have leveled with me when she gave me the amulet. It seems like she set me up to fail."

"Maybe, or perhaps she knew you were too bright to sit back and wait for the other piece of the artifact to come to you. Our mothers were friends, so I'm sure she knew you would be safe as soon as you connected with my family." Bronx wasn't completely convinced he was right, but he hated knowing Kenya's memory of her mother would be forever tainted by deception.

"Thank you for that... I'm still not sure how I feel about all the deception, but I can let some of the emotion go, knowing she didn't simply throw me to the wolves. Oh, crap on a cracker, talk about stepping in it." She shook her head at her own careless use of words as Bronx chuckled softly. Taking a deep breath, she let herself relax more into Bronx's hold and felt his cock stir against her. "Audric asked me to wait until I have all the information before I pass judgment, and I know I promised I would, but it's really hard... Oh, my heavens."

"*Cheŕ*, you said the magic word. It is indeed *hard*. Lean forward, put your palms on the wall with your fingers splayed." She didn't hesitate, knowing the distraction was going to be worth the effort. "Spread your legs as far apart as you can, mate. Yes, perfect. Now, turn your toes in and push that beautiful ass out for me." She expected him to push into her. Instead, he smoothed his soap and slickened hands up her legs. By the time his hands reached her hips, the bubbles had swirled their way down the drain, leaving his fingers free of soap as he moved them to the inside of her thighs.

Using his thumbs, Bronx spread the soft globes of her ass cheeks, baring her rear hole to his view. Tracing the pad of one finger around the tight muscle guarding another slice of heaven, he smiled when she moaned.

"I'm looking forward to claiming your ass, Kenya."

"I haven't ever... I don't think you will fit... too big." Her head was swimming, her brain slowly shutting out anything resembling reason as it was taken over by white-hot desire, burning her from the inside out. She'd just started to believe Bronx was her fated mate when Audric's earlier revelations fanned the spark of self-doubt, always lurking just below the surface.

Inside, she was still the chubby little girl other kids loved teasing by fooling her into thinking one of the most popular girls in school was her friend. Kenya remembered the humiliation as though it was yesterday. She'd been so excited, telling her mother about all the things she and her new best friend were going to do together. Then she'd gone to school earlier than usual the next day, excited to spend time with her new friend. Instead of a chance to chat with her new friend, she overheard the girl laughing with her 'group' about how easy it had been to dupe the fat girl with the ratty clothes. She'd only been nine or ten years old, but it was a lesson Kerya had never forgotten.

"I'm going to keep telling you until you believe me—fate never makes a mistake. If you don't stop letting your mind wander into minefields, I'm going to turn this luscious ass scarlet, and it won't be the erotic spanking I think you'd enjoy." *Enjoy? Is he nuts? Why would anyone enjoy being beaten?* "Spanked, not beaten, *Chef*. You have a lot to learn about dominance and submission. I'll be patient during the learning curve, but I want you to keep an open mind as you learn."

"As I was walking out to meet Tobi and Gracie, I read a large poster on the wall that mentioned safe words." It was easier for her to talk about things when he wasn't staring into the very depths of her soul. Damn, the man had the most intense gaze she'd ever encountered. Of course, that wasn't saying much since the one thing she missed the most living on the street was having people look her in the eye. It was sad the way people look through you as if you weren't there.

"Prairie Winds is part of a network of clubs, and their reputation for safety is second to none. Kent and Kyle are devoted to the safety of every member and guest, but they are particularly focused on the submissives. Every Dominant in the club is charged with ensuring the absolute safety of every submissive. If a sub says the word red, you'll see people come out of the woodwork to make certain the scene stops. If the sub doesn't feel safe or comfortable talking things through with the Dom, there are several other options available. I've even seen members of the club's security team drive subs home if there was any doubt about their safety."

"If the Wests are Doms, why didn't they marry a submissive? Tobi and Gracie are so successful, I can't imagine them letting anyone boss them around." It was a question she'd been struggling with since she'd met the two women. Bronx had been sliding his fingers through her slick folds, ratcheting up her desire so fast, she was sure this would be the last coherent question she would be able to form before her brained switched off. *Hell, at this point, I'll be lucky if I can make heads or tails from his answer.*

"It takes a strong woman to admit what she needs. Tobi and Gracie are both subs. I think you are confusing sexual submission with being a doormat. I assure you the subs at Prairie Winds are some of the strongest women you'll ever meet." His words started floating around the room in random patterns, making them impossible to grasp. She heard him chuckle as he pressed the tip of his cock against her opening. "*Cher*, you are a wonder. Your mind is a mystery, I'm looking forward to spending the rest of our lives exploring."

Kenya's body was miles ahead of her mind when it came to her sexual response to Bronx. The flash of heat from the stretch of the tender tissues of her vagina strained in their attempt to accommodate his girth. *Why does he feel even bigger now? Is that even possible? I probably should have paid closer attention during that damned freshman human sexuality class.* If he responded, she didn't hear it because every bit of her focus was centered on the incredible sensation of Bronx thrusting himself as deep into her pussy as he could go. The rigid ring of his corona pressed against her G-spot with each pass, making her legs tremble, her heart threatening to vibrate out of her chest as her orgasm thundered through her.

"Holy fuck. So hot. Wet, silken heat washing over my cock, testing every bit of my control—you are a gift from Freya. Goddess above, your vice grip on me is heaven and hell, two sides of the same coin and more than I could have ever hoped for." Kenya recognized the name. Freya was magic's answer to Aphrodite and Isis. Hearing Bronx refer to her as a gift from a deity as revered as Freya made Kenya's heart clench in response. As a student of magical history, she understood the significance of his comparison and couldn't imagine a bigger compliment.

It took Kenya several minutes to become cognizant enough to notice Bronx was still blanketing her back. She welcomed his body heat radiating over her sweat-cooled back. With one arm wrapped around her torso, anchoring her to his chest, Kenya didn't know how he had the strength to hold himself up with one arm.

Reading about the physical strength and speed of shifters hadn't prepared her for the reality. Bronx had promised her she'd experience many of the physical benefits after he claimed her, but so far, the most noticeable change was her hearing. It had already improved exponentially, almost to the point of being overwhelming. She was relieved when the enhancement slowed to a more manageable level. She was starting to understand why people were so stressed all the time—damn, the world surrounding them was loud and annoying.

Chapter Thirteen

B RONX SHOOK HIS head as he tried to get his bearings. Fucking hell, he'd always hated magical travel, and time travel was even more disorienting. Anyone prone to motion sickness was particularly susceptible and usually passed up offers to circumvent traditional travel options. Kenya's obvious reluctance was the reason he'd opted to go first, tagging Kenya and Audric to pull them along behind him. Bronx wanted to be ready to help her get her bearings once she and Audric arrived.

"Holy hell in the Highlands, where are we?" Bronx could hear Kenya's excited voice but had trouble seeing her through the thick foliage. Didn't it figure she'd weathered the trip without any issues while his head was still spinning like a damned top?

"We are about a half-mile from the clearing. I wanted to make certain you weathered the trip without becoming ill." Audric's calm voice sounded from a few yards to Bronx's left.

It didn't matter there was a full moon, the sacred light wasn't able to penetrate the thick tree canopy. Crystal clear night vision was one of the shifter traits Bronx found the most useful. The minute he saw Kenya, he knew she'd already noticed the difference. It only took him a few steps to reach her side, and he didn't waste any time pulling her against his side.

"I can see everything. This is kick-ass, I tell you. Absolutely amazing." A quick glance at Audric and he knew the other man was amused by the wonder in Kenya's voice. "I can hear all the little creatures scurrying around... okay, maybe that isn't necessarily a good thing, but it's still a huge change. It had to be so cool growing up being able to see at night. Good grief, you had to have felt so much safer. One of the worst parts of being hearing impaired while living on the streets was the fear someone could sneak up on me. It's one of the reasons I enjoyed sleeping in your offices. Shoot, I'll just stop chattering like a magpie now."

"You are such a breath of fresh air, Kenya." Audric's amused chuckle sounded from in front of them. They'd already agreed Audric would lead them to their destination since he'd been seen a portion of the original ceremony. He'd told them his vantage point hadn't allowed him to see how many pieces had been created or who they'd been given to, so he was leading them to a spot where they'd have a much better view. "We're early, but we'll need to be in place well before the others arrive, so we need to move along."

They made their way through the forest, passing close enough to a cottage, Bronx was able to make out many of the architectural details of the small stone structure, surprised by its storybook appearance. It wasn't long before they passed a much larger structure. This house was the original portion of Bronx's sister-in-law, Vienna's family home. He'd heard plenty about the house and the underground vault, so he was pleased when Auric led them around the outside entrance to the cave beneath the house. In later years, the secondary entrance would be hidden by a greenhouse, but they'd traveled to a time at least a hundred years before recorded history would begin documenting details of the property.

In the distance, Bronx made out cloaked figures walking single file parallel to the path they were following. The small group wasn't making any attempt to be quiet, their words easy to hear.

"Stafford's gunning for a seat on the Council. We must get this done before he shows up. He will insist we summon a Council member, and we do not have time for such a delay." The words were spoken by the man leading the group through the woods. The man was carrying a torch, so Bronx assumed he wasn't a shifter.

"We must not let him get his hands on the talisman."

"Never. We cannot allow him to secure his seat by stealing what does not belong to him."

"Our plans are too important." The comment piqued Bronx's curiosity, and he hoped Audric would be able to explain what the women meant.

"I am tired of the Council controlling our every move. Soon they will dictate every spell we use." *Good Goddess, some things never change. Hell, people are still fighting against being controlled by those in power.* "In a few years, we will have enough power to break away from their control with this totem." The woman speaking sounded enough like Vienna, Bronx suspected this was the woman responsible for so much sorrow in his new sister's life.

Bronx could tell by Audric's reaction he recognized the

voices. Damn, he hoped none of them turned out to be his own ancestors. How embarrassing would that be? Bronx could see the clearing Audric had said the group planned to use. The elderly wizard's memory was remarkable. He'd described the area perfectly, down to the knotted tree they were crouched behind. Audric waved his hand in a circle above his head, leaving a trail of floating pieces of glitter that quickly took the shape of a dome over the three of them.

"It's going to take them a few minutes to set everything up, so I've covered the three of us in a dome of silence, so you're free to ask questions without worrying about being heard."

"Damn, you are amazing, Mr. ... I mean, Audric. And smart, too, since my voice always seems too loud. I never really mastered the art of whispering." Kenya sighed and shrugged her shoulders. "Guess I'm not great at the whole staying on topic or shutting up when I should either."

"Talking when you are nervous is perfectly natural, Kenya. It's also a habit you'll likely outgrow as your self-confidence grows." Bronx watched her eyes widen in surprise, making him sad. Shit, hadn't anyone ever paid her a damned compliment?

"They will set up five fires at the points of a pentagram you see marked with stones. This location is one they've used many times for various coven gatherings, but the land has recently been sold, and it's the last time they will be allowed to use this location. One of the younger witches is married to the man who bought the property. He is an elder in the local church and doesn't know his new wife is a witch."

"Does he ever find out?"

"Not until after she poisons him. She tells him as he lies dying in their bed. I've tried to keep an open mind and not hold it against her. After all, he was a hideous hypocrite and mean as a snake. The woman you heard speaking is her mother. She was as power-hungry as any magical I've ever known. No one shed a tear when she mysteriously vanished a few years after the ceremony." He turned to look at the group gathering a few yards away before continuing.

"The daughter is a member of the Magic Council—has been for many years. She is looking forward to meeting Vienna in the near future." Audric turned back to the group, watching as more people joined those building what looked like small teepees of wood. In the center, they spread a large, round tattered piece of cloth over the grass, then set a fabric wrapped object in the center. The young woman who pushed her hood down to expose long auburn curls looked so much like Vienna's, it was startling.

"Yes, Esmerelda is Vienna's great-grandmother. Her mother is the angry-looking woman behind her. Not all the witches who took part in this ceremony wanted to over-throw the Council. Essie knew the piece you're going to see was too powerful for any one person to have in their possession. Power of that magnitude can corrupt even the purest heart."

Esmerelda pulled a shiny fabric ribbon from around the package and let the material fall away, exposing the totem they planned to split apart.

Bronx gasped when he saw what everyone was calling one of the most powerful magical icons ever created.

"Catalina has one of these in her front window display."

"Yes, she does. The Magic Council started getting calls about it as soon as it was unveiled." Audric's response shocked him.

"Is that why you talked to her yesterday?"

"No, we had already had several enlightening conversations prior to the one yesterday. Just so you know, she has a fascinating story to tell you all about how her design came to be. Your sister is a remarkable artisan; no one should be surprised the other side chose her to help them."

"She's a conduit, isn't she? The other side talks to her." Bronx enjoyed watching Kenya's eyes dance with knowledge as she put together pieces of the puzzle. It shouldn't surprise anyone she'd made education a priority, even at the expense of having a place to live.

"Until recently, Catalina had no idea where her ideas were coming from—she'd never associated the voices in her head as anything other than her creativity speaking out loud." Audric turned to check what was happening in the meadow. Bronx wondered what he was waiting for but didn't want to ask a question that would sidetrack the conversation. "We see this same form of magic with writers. They believe it's their imagination speaking the words onto the page when, in fact, it is a voice or voices from the other side. Just because a soul moves to the other side of the veil, it doesn't stop creating, and it certainly doesn't want to be silenced. Some of the greatest authors of all time were merely channeling the stories they were hearing."

"I hate to admit it, but hearing this is kind of a relief. It was always a little depressing when other students would

all he needed to feel grounded.

"Look closely at the totem, and you'll be able to see power shimmering around it, much like the auras we see surrounding people. The effect is the same. Everything is made up of energy. Mankind has made many advances in the identification of the particles involved, but it's knowledge magicals have been using for centuries."

They watched what looked like a small, sculptured piece of metal shimmer brightly against the black velvet backdrop of the forest. The five small fires provided little more than a glimmer of light, something Bronx suspected was intentional.

One of the witches poured a small flask of amber liquid into the mortar, the contents flashing a blinding white light, illuminating the entire meadow for no more than a split second, but it was long enough for a man on the other side of the group to lock his eyes on the spot where they stood. It was only then Bronx realized Audric had dropped the privacy dome. The man's attention was immediately focused on Kenya, and Bronx's arms tightened around her as he felt his wolf stirring beneath the surface.

Listening as the group began chanting in what Bronx recognized as Latin, he strained to put together the few words he recognized.

Let the light of the moon's magic shine on each piece as it travels forth. Each part of a whole... together they make something greater than the sum of the parts. Audric's interpreted words floated through Bronx and Kenya's minds.

"Synergy." Kenya's whispered word so quietly, Bronx had barely been able to hear it, and there wasn't a breath of air separating the two of them. Audric turned to her and nodded.

"Synergy is one of the least appreciated properties of energy. It's what your generation calls a game-changer. That's why the pieces your ancestors have worn since this night are small and don't appear to be particularly powerful."

Bronx suspected Audric was deliberately distracting them with pieces of fluff. Stafford hadn't attained his position in the magic world by giving away secrets. Even though Bronx liked and respected the man, he wasn't going to forget Audric had an agenda, and in the end, that would be what took precedence.

Chapter Fourteen

Kenya felt oddly connected to the ceremony as if she were a part rather than an observer. It was a strange feeling, and the odd sense of association was strengthened when her gaze locked on a man standing just inside the tree-line on the other side of the meadow. He walked among the coven members, but none of them acknowledged his presence—how peculiar. Thanks to her newfound night vision, Kenya saw the man's eyes widen in what looked like recognition. *How is that possible?*

With his eyes locked on her, Kenya felt a magnetic pull toward the man despite the fact they couldn't possibly know one another. As he came closer, she heard Audric's muttered curse from behind her, but she couldn't seem to pull her gaze from the stranger who seemed zeroed in on her.

"I would have recognized you anywhere, Kenya. You are the image of your grandmother. It's remarkable how much you look like my beloved." Standing in front of her, Kenya could see the man's eyes were kinder than they'd appeared at a distance. "You can speak to me, you know. I'm a time traveler, the same as your mate. I've been traveling back to this ceremony every full moon since you moved to Texas, hoping one day you'd be here."

"William, all you needed to do was ask."

"I've already made too many mistakes. I didn't want to risk making another by trusting someone who has no reason to help me." For the first time, Kenya saw a spark of heat in the man's eyes as his gaze flicked to Audric before returning to her. "Does she know who she is?"

What? What was he talking about?

"We will discuss this later. Right now, we need to make certain we have all the details needed to restore the totem, so it can be returned to the vault for safekeeping."

"You already know there are five pieces, each of the elements of the pentagram, and you know which families end up with the pieces, so why don't you tell Mr. Adler and my granddaughter why you are really here, Stafford. She is the Fitzpatrick heir and deserves to know the power of her position."

"Granddaughter?" Kenya felt like someone had just kicked her in the chest. How could she have a grandfather no one had ever told her about? Why would her mother be so cruel? It boggled the imagination.

Don't fall into a pit of questions just yet, there will be plenty of time for that later.

Bronx felt Kenya stiffen in his arms and knew he was treading on thin ice. Hell, he'd essentially told her to *calm down,* and he'd dealt with his sisters enough to know those were fighting words.

Hell hath no fury like a woman told her anger should

be set on the back burner. When Bronx felt her shaking in his arms, he turned her to face him so quickly, she lost her balance, falling against his chest. Before he could set her back on her feet, he heard tinkling laughter and felt relief wash over him.

"Remind me to thank your sisters for making you self-aware. I'm sure they've done a wonderful job of preparing you for mating."

He'd have been thrilled to hear her finally referring to them as mates if he hadn't known her words were pure sarcasm. Israel had been listening in on his thoughts their entire lives—you'd think he'd be used to it—but Bronx was still trying to adjust to Kenya being able to hear his thoughts as clearly as he heard hers.

"I'm sure they'll be happy to regale you with plenty of exaggerated tales of their invaluable guidance." Bronx sighed and shook his head before continuing, "They're a lively group, and my sisters-in-law fit in perfectly. You've gained a rather large family in a short amount of time—I hope like hell they don't overwhelm you."

"The Adlers are indeed a large family, but you also have another large group to call your own, Kenya. The Fitzpatricks are a huge clan, and they've been waiting a long time to meet you." Before any of them could respond to William's comment, a brilliant flash of green light illuminated the entire area. *Goddess above, the glow was probably visible from the space station.* It took him a few seconds to realize why Kenya was shaking with laughter again. Rolling his eyes at his own timeline blunder, Bronx returned his attention to the activity in the meadow.

The magical artifact resting in the center of the pentagram was vibrating at such a high frequency, he and Kenya both gasped as they worked frantically to cover their ears. Both wizards waved their hands at the same time, their magic combining to seal the four of them under a transparent dome, silencing the din that had made his ears hurt bad enough, he hoped like hell they weren't bleeding.

"Sorry, I forgot about your enhanced hearing. Remember, they are separating a piece made from metal and magic." Audric's sheepish expression made Bronx roll his eyes. You could bet your ass he'd have remembered if it was his ears ringing from the beating they'd taken.

"I've seen the way your generation separates metal. Burning things into pieces is barbaric and changes all the properties at the edges where the flame cuts through the metal like a hot knife through butter." Kenya turned to him, confusion lighting her eyes.

"What the hell is he talking about?" Bronx almost laughed out loud at the mortified look Kenya's question elicited in William Fitzpatrick's expression.

"A cutting torch. I'm not sure when or where a two-hundred-year-old wizard would have had occasion to see one in action, but there it is."

"Don't ever underestimate your elders, Mr. Adler. We've seen and heard almost everything, and we have low bullshit thresholds. Magicals who continue learning live longer than those who sit on their laurels, watching the world spin around them. I knew your parents, and contrary to what many people would have you believe, they were keenly aware they'd been targeted—and they knew why."

The knowledge in Fitzpatrick's eyes was quickly shuttered, leaving Bronx wondering what information Kenya's grandfather could share. What part, if any, had Fitzpatrick played in his mom and dad's death.

Shaking his head, William's shoulders dropped. "I wouldn't have ever hurt them, Bronx." Waving his hand to the group, gathering closer and closer to the artifact, he seemed lost in his own thoughts for several long seconds. "The dark forces that claimed your parents also took my son—he was my world, and I've never stopped grieving." Bronx felt like an ass but knew any attempt to apologize would sound condescending, making the situation worse rather than healing the damage his careless assumption had done.

"Look closely at the people in front of you." Audric leaned close to Kenya, his knotted finger pointing to the group in front of them. "I'm not sure how many people you'll recognize since you haven't been exposed to as many magicals as your mate, but I suspect the pictures in your history books will give you some background." As soon as Bronx focused his attention on the faces rather than their actions, he was shocked to realize he recognized several people.

"That's you, isn't it? Oh, my… what do you want me to call you? Mr. Fitzpatrick seems too formal, and grandfather seems presumptuous. Heck, you might decide you don't want to know me at all when you get to know me."

All three men stared in shock at Kenya, unable to believe what they were hearing. William surprised Bronx when he was the first to recover enough to speak.

"I'd be honored if you called me grandfather, Kenya. Your father never stopped looking for you. We never knew who was helping your mother with the spells required to hide you from us. Lisa's magical skill was limited. She simply wasn't gifted enough to do the magic required."

Kenya nodded her understanding, but Bronx sensed she didn't know who'd been helping her mom. If he had to guess, Bronx was going with Lisa tapping into her daughter's magic for the additional power.

It seemed to him Kenya spent her entire childhood trying to catch up—about the time she would get her feet under her, her mom would pack them up and move, forcing her daughter to begin the whole process again. Her mother kept her off-balance with the moves and siphoning off her magic.

"The answer to your question is, yes, I was here to claim one of the pieces of the artifact for my family. I'm sure it will look familiar." The older man's expression softened as his gaze centered on the pendant resting snugly at the base of her throat. She traded the longer chain for a much shorter one at Bronx's request. He'd had been concerned the longer links could become tangled as they time traveled, and he wouldn't risk her safety.

When Bronx suggested they leave both of their pendants in the vault in Catalina's store, Audric shook his head, insisting even without the other pieces, they would offer an additional layer of protection. Knowing they needed every bit of protection available had made him wish Kenya would reconsider the trip, but she'd been insistent, and the truth was, he had no legitimate argument against her claim that she had as much right to be there as he did.

Kenya turned to Audric, her mouth open to speak when she stopped, tilting her head to the side, and reaching for the elderly man. "Audric, what's wrong?" Bronx turned to see the older man's eyes glassy with unshed tears.

"You see the woman with dark red hair?" He and Kenya nodded as William set his hand atop Audric's shoulder in an obvious show of support. "That is my Elizabeth, Charlotte's grandmother. Lizzy gave Charlotte the pendant to her just a few days before she passed."

"It's my understanding the pieces have all been passed down a short time before the owner dies—it's as if they know their time is nearing an end." The whole thing was starting to become borderline creepy in Bronx's view. He was looking forward to putting the entire mess behind them. For the first time, Bronx understood why his brothers had been so anxious to claim their women as mates and wives and was grateful he'd already made Kenya his own.

Keeping his focus on the ritual playing in front of them was becoming impossible as pictures from Kenya's mind began floating through his own. Damn, his mate was replaying her claiming and the explosive sex they'd had both before and after. When he dialed it in, Bronx was able to feel her emotions along with hints of the physical sensations she'd experienced as he pushed his cock balls deep in her heated pussy.

Before this moment, Bronx would have told you nothing could feel better than the intimate flesh of her wet velvet heat rippling over the sensitive skin covering his cock. But now? Experiencing it from her point of view was running a close second. Grateful he'd learned a long time ago how to block others from eavesdropping, Bronx felt his cock pressing against the unrelenting steel of his zipper and sent up a silent prayer to Goddess charged with making certain his favorite appendage survived the hard-on from hell, his mate's vivid memory caused.

Isolating the two of them telepathically from the others should have been easy, but Bronx was finding it incredibly challenging to maintain the level of concentration required. Worried his mate's intimate thoughts were going to be exposed to the two wizards, he reluctantly tightened his hold enough to pull her back to the moment. Leaning down, letting his breath brush over the sensitive shell of Kenya's ear, he relished her response. Feeling a shiver work itself up the length of her spine made him smile. He could have spoken the words quietly enough for her to hear, but whispering them into her mind was far more intimate.

Unless you want me to pull you into the woods and have my wicked way with you, Cher, you need to tone it down. Those memories are hotter than hell, and feeling it from your side was fucking intense. Unfortunately, I need some of my blood flowing to my brain rather than pooling much farther south. The little minx snaked a hand behind her to grasp him through the denim covering his straining erection. Sucking in a quick breath, his head and cock began battling about the best course of action, having distinctly different ideas about how he should proceed.

I don't understand why we're here. What difference is it going to make if Audric finds out who got the pieces? He knows who has them now, and I think he knew how many there are. There's more going on here, and I don't know what it is.

Bronx hadn't known either until William walked up to them—what he didn't know was why Audric had taken such a roundabout route to reunite his former friend with his granddaughter.

Refocusing on the small group in the meadow, it was easy to identify the ancestors of his sisters-in-law. Proving how powerful human genetics could be, it was easy to match the witches to the women he now considered family—with one notable exception. None of the participants looked Native American or Alaskan Eskimo. Kensington's wife and mate, Denali, was a product of both sides of her family, but none of the people gathered around the shimmering metal totem resembled either of those indigenous groups.

"No one here is related to Denali." Audric had tuned in to Bronx the moment he'd dropped the shield. "The piece Denali wears represents the water element, and the hand of fate knows nothing of coincidence. Her grandmother found the piece partially buried in the wreckage of a ship along the shore of a small Aleutian Island. The woman you see at the side of the meadow is planning to steal the pendant from her sister. It's an age-old story of lost or stolen love, depending on your point of view."

"Who is Denali? I thought it was a place, not a person." Bronx smiled at the two men as he turned Kenya, so he could look into her eyes as he answered.

"Says the woman named Kenya?" Realization brightened her eyes, and he looked forward to seeing her smile more often... naked. Oh yeah, naked and smiling was a great plan. "Denali is my sister-in-law. She is married to my brother, Kensington. He rescued her when she was thrown off a bridge into a freezing cold river."

"Kensington? The actor Kensington Adler is your brother? Why didn't I know this? Nobody ever tells me anything. My mother kept me under a damned rock, and now I look like a blooming idiot every time I turn around. This frosts my cookies. How many Adlers are there? I know you said it was a big family, but no one mentioned movie stars. Damn... _et me guess, there are Nobel Prize winners and famous singers, too." All three men were staring at her Kenya in disbelief before William's booming laughter broke the silence.

"Damn, she's a Fitzpatrick, alright." William waved a hand, covering them in a shower of glitter. What the hell was with wizards and glitter? Bronx was never going to get that shit out of his hair "Take her home. We've drawn too much attention. I'll make sure Audric gets back. We'll meet you in Texas tomorrow, and we'll come to the front door."

Bronx understood what Kenya's grandfather was saying, but he could see his mate's frustration slowly morphing into confusion—her bewildered expression the last thing he saw before he pulled her against his chest and whispered the short incantation sending them hurtling back through the tunnel of time.

Watching the brilliant bands of color fly past as they slid along the tube had begun to feel old hat before he mated with Kenya. Now that he'd traveled with her, seen the look of wonder in her eyes as they raced back to the present, Bronx once again understood how truly remarkable his gift was.

"I still have trouble believing this is real." He wasn't sure if she'd spoken the words aloud or if he was becoming so attuned to her, he was hearing her thoughts without realizing the communication was telepathic. "If I hadn't experienced it, I'd have never believed it was possible." She turned her face to his and grinned. "You have to admit, this is totally dope." He must have looked confused because she giggled, "Sorry. I picked up some of the younger student's slang whenever I could afford to take classes. I'm probably woefully out of date now. I hope I can find a job soon. Even with a steady paycheck, it will take me a while to save up enough money for tuition." Looking around her, Kenya seemed shocked to discover they were sitting on his sofa in front of the fire.

"It's a huge turn-on to know you are so focused on our conversation, you've blocked out everything else, but it also makes me worry for your safety." As Kenya became more acclimated to her new shifter traits, Bronx was convinced her situational awareness would become more acute, but after someone fired shots at the house, he wasn't willing to take any chances with her safety. He only hoped once the pieces of the magical icon were once again joined together and the Council of Magic had the powerful metal sculpture tucked away in a vault, the danger to Kenya would be over.

"We're going to have a long chat about you enrolling in college. If you want to finish, we'll make it happen. Hell, I might even be able to work in a couple of schoolgirl scenes at the club. This is a conversation we'll be having… later." Several hours later, if he had his way. "First, we're going to make some new memories to go along with the hot ones you were sharing with me in front of two of the oldest—not to mention, most powerful—wizards in the world." Scooping her up in his arms, Bronx stalked down the hall toward what he now considered *their* bedroom.

Her laughter and squeals of delight were music to his

ears. Getting her alone was a blessing; getting inside her would save his sanity. As close as he could figure it, he'd have her naked and in the shower in under ninety seconds. Add another ninety to make certain she was ready for him. Perfect. He'd be buried as deep as he could go, her toned legs wrapped around his waist in three minutes or less.

Chapter Fifteen

A UDRIC LOOKED AT William and grinned. "Just like old times, my friend. I appreciate you sending the kids home. I never intended for their safety to be compromised."

"I know why they were here, and they'll figure it out soon enough." William looked at the frozen scene in front of them. As soon as Bronx pulled Kenya into the time tunnel, Audric whispered the words that stopped everything taking place in the meadow—even the flames were paused.

William had to admit the man's command of magic was damned impressive. Letting his gaze settle on the much younger version of his wife, William felt his eyes well with tears. He'd thought losing his son was the most difficult thing he would ever have to endure, but he'd been wrong.

Watching his beloved, Isla, fade into a slow death had drained him in ways he'd never imagined possible. In the end, he'd been grateful she was no longer in pain—but William learned the depth of sorrow and how lost he felt without her. "I know I told Kenya she has a large family on the Fitzpatrick side, and it's true there is a rather impressive number of extended members of the clan."

"But she is the only family you have left, my friend... and it was time. Pretending you didn't know where she was because you were afraid of being rejected was never going to get you what you really wanted. I know we've had our disagreements over the years, but it's time to set all that aside." Reaching out to grasp William's forearm, Audric infused the connection with warm energy, letting it seep all the way to his friend's soul. "I know it was difficult to resist using magic to ease her suffering. Doing what's right is rarely easy. We are often overly optimistic when our souls come to this world for lessons. Letting her spirit suffer so it could grow and advance to higher levels was a lesson for all of us."

"She insisted on coming with me to this ceremony." William chuckled at the memory. "Damn, she was a stubborn woman. When she found out I was the only man planning to attend, she flew into a rage."

"You were quite the catch, and she damned well wasn't letting you slip away." Audric's words were accompanied by a warm smile, reflecting amusement rather than judgment.

"I knew her family was a source of embarrassment for her. Those who choose the dark side of magic never consider the way their decisions taint the other members of their family."

Shortly before Isla came of age, her family's choices made them outcasts in the magical community. The scandal almost derailed her engagement to William, the entire mess something she'd never gotten over. Shaking his head, William turned to the man who'd once been his closest friend. It was time to set all the old competition aside.

"Enough of this, we already know there are only five pieces, but neither one of us can remember the spell used to separate the elements into the medallions our descents have been wearing."

"Once we hear it again, figuring out how to reverse it should be easy. None of the women will be safe until the icon is reassembled and safely stored in the vault."

Audric was right about what it would take to ensure the women's safety, and William hoped it would be as simple as the man standing next to him implied.

"Getting older is a pain in the ass. I helped with the spell and can't remember the details. It's damned humbling."

"The alternative has some serious drawbacks as well. Besides, look at the bright side—we've lived long enough, people expect us to say outrageous shit, so we can speak our minds without worrying about the consequences. Naps are perfectly acceptable, we can wear comfortable clothes, and no one bitches about our fashion choices."

William couldn't hold back his laughter. "Hellfire, you're right. I've been looking at this thing all wrong."

"Earth, Wind, Fire, Water, and Life Force. Magical elements that make up the energy of the Universe." They listened to the incantation, rewinding the scene twice to make sure they'd gotten all the details. "I recorded this with the snazzy phone Charlotte got me for my birthday, but I'll be damned if I can figure out how to get anything back on the stupid thing."

"Will it work? Taking it back to the present?" William

could think of at least a dozen reasons it shouldn't—but in the world of magic, things were rarely what they seemed.

"Sure... well, for me. I made sure I didn't capture myself on film."

"Phones don't use film, you dolt."

"Fuck you. I suppose you're one of those... damn, what do they call the lunatics who think everything should be digital?"

"Geniuses?"

"Tell me again why we were friends." Audric's words sounded gruff, but his eyes were dancing with mischief. "Techy. That was the word Charlotte used. Gigi will be able to find the damned video if we need help remembering anything."

William laughed as they set the scene in motion again as he waved his hand, sending them hurtling down through the tube of time. He'd gotten used to the sensation of being hurtled through space, but Audric was looking a bit worse for wear. When they landed outside one of his favorite Irish pubs, Audric looked over at William and chuckled.

"You buying? Damn I haven't been here in a hundred years."

"I'll buy the fish and chips—you buy the booze. I doubt your tastes have gotten any cheaper or your control any better." William didn't move to the door, giving Audric a minute or two to gather his senses. No need to stagger in the door when it was almost certain they'd be staggering out in a couple of hours.

"You still have an apartment down the street?" Audric shook his head, snorting a laugh as he took in the gas street lamps and Victorian dresses and suit coats of the couples walking by. "Time travel always did confuse the hell out of me. Come on, I really need a drink. We don't have to be back in Texas for…"

This time it was William who laughed. Shaking his head, he slapped his hand atop Stafford's shoulder and steered his friend toward the pub's entrance. William could take them to any point time, so it didn't matter how long they spent in Dublin. He had a feeling neither of them was going to feel up to sliding through a brightly colored tube at Mach speed anytime soon.

<hr />

BRONX LET THE tip of his cock slip through the outer lips of Kenya's pussy and groaned when he found her slick with arousal. "Fucking perfect, *Cher*. We'll do sweet and sensual later. This round it's going to be hard and fast. Hang on to my shoulders, mate."

"Yes. Hard is good. Really hard is even better. Don't worry about fast. I'm going to come as soon as you push in. Oh, God, please fuck me." Her hands were gripping the tops of his shoulders so tight, he could feel her nails sharpening and wondered if she realized how close she was to shifting.

"I'm going to put you over my knee for topping from the bottom after we have a long chat about the rules, but right now, I'm happy to oblige."

With water cascading down on them from the rain showerhead, Bronx couldn't take his eyes off the woman who held his heart in the palm of her hand. Damn, he loved seeing her eyes outlined by glistening water droplets clinging to her lashes as the blue orbs glazed over with passion. He knew he'd never forget this moment or the sound of her voice as she begged him to fuck her.

Thrusting his hips forward, Bronx pushed through the heat of her pussy until his tip was pressed against the opening of her cervix. Kenya's shudder started in her core, then slowly worked itself around his aching erection before quaking to the surface. Pressing her back to the smooth marble wall, Bronx slid his arms under her knees, hooking them over his elbows. The shift in position opened her up even farther to his thrusts, and Bronx didn't waste any time giving her what both their bodies craved.

Hearing her soft sighs become louder, more urgent pleas for more was music to his ears. There was a deeper tone to her voice, bordering on the growl of her wolf. Bronx didn't miss it, but since he could hear how scrambled her thoughts were becoming, he doubted she'd noticed. Her body was slowly adapting to the genetic changes, and he was grateful for the more relaxed pace, considering all the other craziness surrounding their mating.

He easily controlled the pace, slowing each time he felt her getting close to tipping over the edge. He wouldn't deny her orgasm, but he damned well wanted the two of them to come together.

"Don't come until I give you permission, *Cher*, I want this to last. Fucking you is melting my mind. Smelling your arousal tests my control in ways you can't possibly imagine. Your scent calls to my wolf, blanking out everything but my need to make you mine in every way possible. Before the night is over, I plan to slide my cock between your sweet lips and claim your luscious ass as well."

Kenya's entire body clenched around him, her nails puncturing his skin as she exhibited the first stages of a shift. He could hardly wait to see what she looked like in her wolf. Seeing the amber lighting her eyes drew his own wolf closer to the surface. Bronx was looking forward to the coming full moon and having the opportunity to claim her wolf by the edge of the lake. He hoped like hell the two wizards weren't planning their ceremony for the same time. If those two old farts fucked up a round of outdoor sex with Kenya, Bronx was going to be pissed.

"Outdoor sex sounds great, but right now, I don't dare think about it. I'm going to come if I think about you taking me outside." Bronx would have laughed at her confession if he hadn't heard the note of desperation in her voice.

"If you come without permission, I'll paddle your ass." Her pussy flooded with warm cream, her arousal bathing his cock in heat. "I think you like the idea of being over my knees, my handprints colored bright red against your alabaster skin. We're going to experiment with that edge of pain, *Cher*, but do yourself a favor and make it an erotic spanking, not a punishment." He didn't want to set her up for failure, so it was time to get both of them to the tipping point.

"Sir? Do you want me to call you, Sir? Anything? Please. I'm going to lose this battle." Kenya's plea was all it took to spur him on.

"Hang on to me, *Chef*. We're going to kick this up a notch. Come as soon as you're ready—I'm going to be right behind you." He wouldn't let go until he knew she'd gotten what she needed—he'd never leave his mate unsatisfied. The one punishment Bronx never used as a Dom was orgasm denial. He'd never met a submissive who didn't resent the hell out of being spun up, then left hanging. The ones he'd talked to assured him it became a trust issue, and he'd seen it in their eyes during scenes. Bronx decided years ago, he'd never punish a sub when he was angry and never use pleasure as a weapon.

"This is too much and not enough at the same time. I feel like I'm falling through a hole in the Universe and soaring above the clouds, but most of all, I feel like something inside me is trying to claw its way out, and I'm burning up from the inside out."

It's your wolf, Chef. Focus on me, on the pleasure.

He could feel her wolf beginning to come into itself, but it still wasn't well-formed enough to fully shift. If she tried to force it now, the consequences could be devastating. He'd never seen someone trapped in a partial shift before, but he'd heard enough rumors to know it was a tragedy that usually claimed both mates. Bronx had grown up hearing that one mate rarely survived long after the first passed, but he hadn't fully understood until Kenya.

Two halves of the same soul can't survive being ripped apart once they've been rejoined during mating.

KENYA WAS GOING to lose her mind if Bronx didn't focus. Holy hat racks for homeless bunnies... he seemed to think she was easily distracted, but she was going to have to step up her game if she was going to keep up with his scattered thinking. It was obvious, he'd forgotten she could hear his thoughts, and the more time that passed since his mating bite, the clearer his internal voice sounded in her mind.

Please. I'm begging you. Harder. I need it harder. She hadn't meant to share her thoughts, but Kenya couldn't make her mind focus on anything aside from her need long enough to figure out how to prevent anyone from eavesdropping. The damned mailman could be listening in as far as she knew—or cared.

Bronx growled, the vibrations coming from deep in his chest. The ominous sound made her think his need might be as urgent as her own—that, or he was angry. She pushed the worry aside—no time to worry about that now. His thrusts were coming faster, pressing her incessantly against the marble wall. He took a half step back, just enough to shift his position and change the angle, making certain the rigid ring encircling the flared head of his cock caressed her G-spot with every thrust.

Bronx's small move was all it took to launch her over the edge into a blinding abyss of brilliant lights flashing behind her eyelids. Kenya felt as if she was soaring. Despite blood thundering in her ears, she heard a woman shout Bronx's name. It took several seconds for her to realize she'd been the one screaming her mate's name. *Damn, I'll probably be embarrassed about that later... but right now, I'm just trying to breathe.*

Bronx lowered her legs to the floor of the shower but

held her close. If he'd released her immediately, Kenya would have collapsed into a heap. When he finally stepped back, Bronx caressed her cheek until her eyes met his.

"Are you okay to finish your shower? I just heard my phone sound the alarm for incoming family." She must have looked confused because he gave a shrug and grinned. "They enter their code before crossing the perimeter. They think it shuts down the alarm system—it doesn't. The code changes the alarm to a different tone, telling me who is coming up the drive."

"Why do I get the idea there is more to the story?"

"The second time my sister Asia walked in to find a gun pointed at her, she announced she wasn't coming out again until I fixed the alarm system or started answering my phone."

"Wouldn't it have been cheaper to answer your phone?"

"Sure, but then I'd have to come up with a plausible excuse to avoid whatever social function she was showing up to demand I attend. This way, I know it's her, and I lock the place down, kill the lights, and wait until she gives up and goes back to Austin."

Her soft laughter as she shampooed her hair made her look like a water sprite enjoying an afternoon rain shower. He'd been looking forward to a nice long round of patio sex, but with Austin headed their way, those plans were going to have to wait.

Austin isn't alone. This is a buy one, get two free deal. Get your ass down here. We need to talk.

What the fuck? I don't want to play reindeer games with you assholes. Go away and let me spend time with my new mate.

Damn it all to hell. He was starting to wish he'd harassed his brothers after they claimed their mates rather than letting them enjoy the time all shifters were supposed to be allotted for the process.

Yeah, yeah, yeah. Cry me a river. None of us are happy to be here, either. If you'd get your horny ass down here, we might be able to get ahead of this train wreck before the hungover wizards show up.

Damn it all. Bronx had a mental vision of his plans going up in smoke as he dried off and stalked into his closet. He would set out clothes for Kenya to wear, so she could join them, but if she was picking up on this conversation, he wouldn't blame her for taking her sweet time getting downstairs. Just in case she was entertaining any thoughts of slipping away, he punched in a command on his phone, activating the underground monitors, so they were sensitive to a much lower weight. A single touch outside a window or door would send a message to his phone. Smiling to himself, Bronx pulled on a pair of jeans and a tattered t-shirt and headed down the hall.

BRIGITTE STAFFORD ROLLED her eyes at Israel's telepathic communication. She doubted he'd deliberately tried to hide the communication because he would have known it was futile.

"Israel never tries to hide behind telepathic communication. He rejoices in speaking right into his brothers' and sisters' heads. It's annoying as hell." Gigi raised her brows in surprise at Austin's sudden outburst. The man who'd claimed Gigi's niece, Charlotte, as his wife and mate was notoriously in control.

"It's easier. People,"—Israel gave his older brother a pointed look—"tend to ignore their phones. I'm much harder to set aside if I'm chattering between your ears rather than trying to speak into them."

"That has to be the lamest excuse I've ever heard. What's the problem with you two, anyway? Austin has a baby at home, so his grumpiness might not be so hard to understand if I didn't know he and Charlotte have one remarkable nanny training another one who, by all accounts, is going to be even better. But you,"—she pointed a blood-red polished finger at Israel—"hell, you should still be in the honeymoon stage of your marriage. I swear the two of you need a session under my lash." The horrified looks on Israel and Austin's faces was worth all the lost hours of sleep.

"Fucking hell, that's never happening. One scene during our Prairie Winds training was more than enough." Gigi laughed because she knew Kent and Kyle were adamant every Dominant spent one evening as a submissive, so they understood the dynamic. It had been the longest evening in Brigitte's life.

"What's not happening? And, what the hell was that bullshit about hungover wizards? If you are talking about Audric and William, when Kenya and I left, they were still watching the separation ritual in the meadow. How did they manage to get drunk? There wasn't a bar or anything else for miles." Bronx moved to the kitchen, pulling a beer from the fridge. Turning, he was surprised to find Brigitte grinning at him. "Holy shit, when Israel said there were three of you, I figured it was Kensington or Cleveland. Wait, why aren't you in Mexico, watching over Denali? Why am I asking all these questions, and nobody's giving me any answers?"

"Perhaps if you took a breath, they'd have a chance to answer." Bronx looked up to see Kenya standing at the end of the hall. Dressed in a cropped top that looked like it had been painted on her and a pair of perfectly faded blue jeans, she took his breath away. With the frayed hems framing her pink polished toes, she looked like a fresh-faced teenager.

"Where did those clothes come from? That's not what I left on the bed."

She blinked at him in confusion.

"I left those for her. You tried to dress her like one of the boys to keep your brothers from looking at her." Gigi was leaning casually against the wall, pretending to look at her nails. The low growl her response got from Bronx made Brigitte smile. Shrugging with feigned disinterest, she added, "You're really on a roll lately. Trying to dress your lovely sub in shabby clothes after shagging her in the shower... I swear your reputation as charming is vastly overrated. And all this after dragging her through several centuries and plopping her down in a dark forest? I assume you've figured out my dad used you for a ride and set Kenya up, so she'd meet William."

All three Adler men stood with their mouths gaping open in shock. Kenya was the only one who appeared to be keeping up—her bark of laughter rang through the silence.

"Audric Stafford is your dad? Oh, I'm so happy to meet you." Extending her hand, she never missed a beat. "I'm

Kenya Star. Your dad is the shit."

Gigi was speechless for a few seconds before she re-membered hearing the young people on Kensington's movie set using the same expression when they thought something was really great.

"I'm Brigitte, but my friends call me Gigi. My dad is something else alright... to be honest, I'm starting to think he is going through his second childhood." Turning so she included the men in the conversation, she nodded at Bronx. "I'm sure you're right about where they were when you left, but they detoured to Dublin. Instead of returning to the here and now, they decided to revisit the pub where they wasted so much of their youth."

"How did you find this out? It's not like someone could have texted you. Wait..." Kenya paused, chewing on her lip, her mind spinning so fast, Gigi was becoming dizzy. "That's not possible, is it? A cell phone working back then without cell towers or electricity? It doesn't seem like it would work, but then again, the world of magic seems to color outside the lines without any trouble... so who knows."

Gigi laughed out loud. "Oh, the Adler ladies are going to love you." Gigi knew they would, to the last one, the Adlers—whether they were born into the clan or mated with one of the five brothers—were all smart as whips and as independent as any women she'd ever met. Each had a unique skillset of magic that was amplified by their mate. The whole family was remarkable. It was easy to see why the Magic Council was watching the group so carefully and tapping their skills when they had a challenge one of the Adlers could help with.

Kenya's cheek flushed a deep red as her gaze dropped to the floor. Bronx held out his hand to her and smiled when she moved to him without hesitation.

Hell, if Brigitte spent much more time in Texas, she was going to start thinking about finding a sub of her own, and she didn't have time for a permanent relationship. If her dad didn't stop acting like a damned teenager, she wasn't going to have any free time at all.

What the hell was he thinking taking off when the rumor mill was in high gear. What the old fool needs is a nice calm witch to keep him company—someone with a level head on her shoulders to keep him out of Irish pubs and give him a reason to stay in the present.

"Why don't you give everyone else the Cliff Notes version of all those thoughts, Gigi? Save me the trouble, and it's better they hear it from you." She tended to forget Israel Adler was a gifted telepath, and his brother-in-law was even better. Thank the Goddess, Luke Grayson, and his wife, Brooklyn, still lived in New Mexico.

Doesn't mean I can't hear you, Gigi. Don't make me send Brooklyn to Texas. She's already worried sick about Catalina. I'm not sure how much longer I can keep her home. Knowing her family is ass-deep in alligators is going to be all the excuse she needs.

Gigi wanted to throw her hands up in frustration. This mess was spiraling out of control and her damned sister, Amaya, was too busy worrying about her next yoga class and whether or not her chakras were in balance to help pull their dad back from his drunken foray.

"While you're at it, maybe you could enlighten us about who has decided our mates should hand over their medallions and how many people have died trying to protect the damned things." Israel wanted answers, and he got the distinct impression Brigitte was holding back.

"Personally, I'd like to know why the Council didn't step in a long time ago. Does anyone know if reassembling this magical totem is going to solve the problem because my gut instinct tells me it won't?" Austin's frustration was edging closer to the surface, and Bronx saw Gigi stiffen at their questions.

I'm going to kick Amaya's namaste ass.

Chapter Sixteen

B RONX LISTENED AS Brigitte complained about her father and William Fitzgerald's detour, more than a little curious how she'd known what the old farts were up to. It was clear she was frustrated with the two elderly men, but Bronx found the entire scenario oddly reassuring. There was something to be said for living long enough to annoy your children and grandchildren—although, from the amused look of Kenya's expression, he'd say William wasn't going to face the same tongue lashing.

"Gigi, I don't mean to be disrespectful, but why is it a problem for your dad and my grandfather to have a night of fun?" The question wasn't unreasonable but seemed to take Gigi by surprise. To her credit, Brigitte gave the question careful consideration before answering.

"It's irresponsible at best and bordering on dangerously negligent."

"Maybe I'm obtuse, but I still don't get it. Was there a scheduled meeting or something?" Gigi seemed to deflate, collapsing in a chair and leaning her head back to stare at the ceiling. "Geez, I'm sorry. I didn't mean to upset you. I'm still trying to figure all this out. My view is probably terribly naïve, but it seems like we just need to get everyone together. Reverse the spell, which I'm guessing isn't that difficult since neither wizard looked like they planned to take notes—heck, they barely paid attention when the statue thing started vibrating like the San Andres Fault."

"Kenya, that statue thing represents a power so strong, it's going to require special handling by a group of magicals to transport it to the Council's safe. The meeting isn't until tomorrow night. Kensington wanted to finish up filming, and he wouldn't let Denali travel without him." Austin shrugged as Israel and Bronx laughed.

"What did you expect? Kensington has yet to realize how self-sufficient his bride is." Austin was right, but after Bronx thought about it, he realized that was true of all their wives.

"I agree with Bronx or at least with what he was thinking." Israel flashed him the same grin Bronx had seen his entire life—and it never boded well. Damn, that smile had preceded a lot of weekends spent in their room, grounded from whatever fun outing their parents had planned. "Great Goddess, you have the memory of a wounded elephant. Do you ever remember the fun stuff?"

"You got me into trouble at every turn, brother."

"Will you two stop bickering like a couple of pre-schoolers? I have a wife and child I'd like to get home to. Hell, I still don't know why I'm here if the ceremony isn't until tomorrow." Bronx chuckled when Gigi stared at her niece's husband in shocked disbelief.

"You're here for snack assignments. What should we put you down for? Cookies? Chips and dip? How about a nice relish plate?" This time, Bronx stared in disbelief, but it didn't last long before everyone in the room dissolved into laughter.

"Damn, Kenya, you surprised the hell out of me, and that doesn't happen very often. I agree with Gigi—though I'll deny it if you tell anyone. You're going to be a big hit with our wives and sisters. Well done." Kenya's cheeks blushed the deepest red Bronx had ever seen on a woman, and he couldn't wait to get their company back out the door.

"Okay, I can take a hint, and if the lot of you would focus for more than ten seconds at a time, I'll wrap this up." Gigi looked at Kenya and smiled. "You're right about my dad and William. I was just frustrated with them for having fun when I'm worried about getting this done. To be honest, I need a damned vacation, and I'm just plain pissy." Turning to the Adler men, her expression became more serious.

"Don't take any chances tomorrow. I don't care how you get here, what kind of security you have to employ to do it... just get here. The dark magic forces are working overtime, trying to figure out how to get around the protections we put into place." She paused, and Bronx waited along with his brothers because it was clear she was holding back. Taking a deep breath, Gigi suddenly looked tired, and Bronx could see she was carrying the bulk of the responsibility on her small shoulders.

"There's one more thing. I know Catalina is in the wind looking for Cooper. If you have any way to contact her, let her know she is looking in the wrong place." Bronx noted Gigi was choosing her words carefully and wondered who was behind her reluctance to speak freely. It was unlike her to be so restrained.

Austin and I are wondering the same thing but want to give her a chance to come clean before calling her on it.

"Listen, I know you are chatting about this between you, and I understand why. Trust me, if I wanted to fool your sixth senses, I'd make a much better effort." Bronx didn't doubt she had plenty in her magical arsenal to back up the claim and didn't see any reason to test her.

"Cooper is working with the Council of Magic. I know at first glance it seems like an unlikely alliance, but if you'll stop and think about it, the whole thing makes sense. They needed someone from outside the magic world—someone with a specific skillset who already knew magicals existed and cared enough to help."

Austin raised his brows in surprise before narrowing them. As the oldest, Austin felt a keen sense of responsibility for his siblings and now by extension, their mates. Catalina hadn't admitted Cooper was the one for her, but she was the only one who hadn't accepted it as a foregone conclusion.

"The Council doesn't want me contacting Catalina; they believe I might be a distraction. Can you imagine that?"

"No! You? A distraction? I can't fathom it."

"Sarcasm is a sign of a subpar wit, Austin." Gigi's glare was worse than her bite, and Austin easily shrugged off her criticism. "You'd make a magnificent toad, but Charlotte would wail, and I've always been a sucker for my niece."

"Who's being sarcastic, now?" Austin rolled his eyes at Gigi.

"Touché."

"What's Cam Barnes' stake in this?" Gigi's eyes widened at Israel's question. "Don't play coy, Brigitte. It's not even remotely convincing. Cam has recently developed a very focused interest in the world of magic, and the man never does anything by half measure. Not to mention the fact Cam and Cooper are practically joined at the hip. What one knows, they both know—if one of them has his fingers in a pie, the other has already been served."

"I feel like I should be taking notes for a who's who in the zoo cheat sheet. Not to mention all the... well, catch-phrases. My senior paper is practically writing itself." Once again, Kenya had managed to defuse the tension in the room, and Bronx was beginning to think she might be magically gifted in more ways than she knew. Reading people, understanding their motives, and when they needed a moment to regroup was more difficult than most people were aware of.

"I can't tell you everything I know, but..."

"But you want to help Catalina because this is some kind of test, right?" If Bronx hadn't been standing directly in front of Gigi when he asked the question, he'd have missed the small reactions most people overlooked. He wasn't surprised when her pupils dilated, and he saw her pulse pounding at the base of her throat.

"Catalina is one of the most gifted magicals in a genera-tion. She is an untapped well of power. What is lacking is her belief in herself and the ability to direct the power bubbling up inside her." Gigi paused for several long seconds, rolling the hem of her shirt between her fingers, the first overt *tell* Bronx had seen her exhibit. "If you talk to her, ask her if she has ever read the book, Valley of the Kings? It's very good, even if it is a bit hard to find." Brigitte pushed her shoulders back, pasted on a phony smile, and moved to the door.

"Let's go. I want to get back in time for Marshall's midnight feeding. He and I have long chats about the moon and stars. I can practically hear his little mind soaking it all in. He's the most brilliant baby to have ever been born." Auntie Brigitte was obviously enamored with her great-nephew. Bronx was thrilled for the little man, the more people who loved a child, the better.

"You'll get no argument from me. Let's go." Austin turned to leave, muttering as he stomped to the door. "Israel, you drive. I'm going to start tracking down Catalina and hope like hell she can get to Egypt before Cooper is on the move again. I'm also going to call Cameron Barnes. It seems we need to have a serious chat about him involving my family in ops without giving me a heads up. Retired my ass."

When Bronx returned to the kitchen, he found Kenya sitting at the table, tears streaming down her cheeks as she stared into a tattered box sitting in front of her.

"*Cher*, what's wrong? Where did that box come from?" It hadn't been there when he walked his brothers and Gigi to the car—there was no way he would have missed seeing it.

"I put the dishes in the dishwasher, and when I turned around, it was sitting here. It's the box that was stolen. I know it probably isn't the exact box, but it looks exactly like mine. It even smells musty like mine. It will be a while before I know if everything is here, but..."

Bronx lifted her from the chair, then settled her on his

lap, taking her place in front of a box that looked as if it had survived World War II. He didn't say anything, preferring to give her time to process everything in her own time.

"No matter what happens with the medallion, at least I'll always have her journals. Don't get me wrong, she wasn't always a lousy mother. We had fun... sometimes... well, when she wasn't high. Some people get lighthearted and jovial when they do drugs, but Lisa Star became combative and verbally abusive. Oh, she'd apologize once she sobered up, but I spent a lot of nights locked in my room to avoid her. After puberty, I discovered I could disappear from her view if I concentrated hard enough. It became easier and easier to blend in with my surroundings as I got older. I'd gotten really good at it by the time I broke into your offices."

"Indeed, you do seem to have mastered the skill. I was going crazy trying to figure out how you were getting in and why I couldn't see you. Brooklyn assured me getting in was easy. She shamed me into updating the security systems at all the locations."

"As your new mate, I'm thankful she was looking out for you, but as the homeless person who relied on your offices for a safe place to shower and sleep, I wasn't a fan."

Bronx chuckled softy at Kenya's admission. He knew she had to have been feeling the walls closing in around her and was damned glad he'd found her before she gave up and moved on. He loved hearing her refer to herself as his mate.

"Speaking of mating, I had plans for you before we were interrupted. Come." Setting her on her feet, Bronx wrapped his hand around her delicate wrist, shackling her in his hold. Feeling her pulse kick up several notches was like throwing gas on the fire of his need to take her. Leading her outside, Bronx paused for a moment, lifting his face to pull in a deep breath. He didn't scent any intruders and was grateful for Israel's team adding underground sensors to the property's perimeter. Moving to the sheltered area near the pool, Bronx grabbed one of the large pillows from the sitting area and dropped it at his feet.

"Kneel, *Chef*. I'm going to claim that pretty mouth of yours." She slid gracefully to her knees, eyes glazing over with the heat of desire. Damn, the woman was a dream come true. Within seconds, she'd freed him from the restrictive confines of his jeans. Bronx groaned in relief when his swollen cock slipped out from behind the zipper he was convinced was tattooing itself along his length. Kenya used the tip of her tongue, sliding it slowly along the underside of his erection from the base to the corona.

"Holy mother of all things magical, your mouth is as hot as your sweet pussy." Looking down on his mate, her face bathed in moonlight, eyes hooded with lust was one of the most erotic things he'd ever witnessed. "Breathe through your nose and show me how deep you can go. That's it. Fuck, yeah. Now, swallow around me." Bronx felt his eyes roll so far back, it was a wonder he didn't see his brain. Hell, maybe it was a good thing he couldn't see all those cells frying from the blazing heat of her mouth.

The energy surrounding her was spiraling up so fast, Bronx felt the hair on his arms standing up straight. The electricity in the air crackled, and he watched as pinpoints of light swirled around them. He shouldn't have been surprised by the rapid increase in her magic ability after hearing his parents talk about how they magnified each other's power, but this was so much more than he'd expected, all he could do was stare in wonder.

"Are you enjoying this as much as I am, *Chef*?" She didn't remove her mouth from his engorged cock, but her deep moan of assent vibrated around him as her scent filled the air around them. "It's fucking hot, knowing you are going to come from giving me pleasure. Come as soon as you can. When I come down your throat, I want you to swallow every drop." He'd barely finished speaking when her mouth tightened around him, her throat massaging him as she swallowed.

Bronx knew she was coming, the shift in energy unmistakable. The combined sensations of her mouth and release were more than enough to shatter his control. It felt like lightning burst from his balls, boiling everything in its path as it raced up his spine, leaving a trail of pleasure in its wake before rocketing back down. The first pulses of seed were painful in their intensity, and for a few seconds, he worried his knees were going to buckle, leaving him in a crumpled heap on the concrete pavers. When the blood stopped thundering in his ears, Bronx realized he'd pushed his fingers into her hair, his grip tighter than would be comfortable now that the heat of the moment had passed.

"Sorry, sweetness. You undid me." Finger combing her tangled locks away from her face, he smiled down into her lust-clouded eyes. Lifting her to her feet, Bronx pulled her against his chest. Wrapping his arms around her, he felt his cock come back to life, clamoring for more. "Come on, let's get inside, you tempting little vixen. I want you to rest a bit before we start on round three." Relief came off her in small waves, and he made a mental note to make certain she understood the importance of letting him know how she felt. It would take a while for her sexual endurance to match his. As a new shifter, her body was still adapting to the changes.

Walking inside, he felt a wave of emotion move over him. The origin was so distant, it was difficult for him to decide if the emotion was anticipation or fear. The one thing he knew for certain, the feeling was coming from someone he knew—someone important to him. Now he needed to figure out who and how he could help.

You already did. I love you, big brother. He'd recognize Catalina's voice anywhere. He couldn't hold back his smile when he saw tears of appreciation in Kenya's eyes.

"I'm anxious to meet the rest of your family. You have no idea how grateful I am for... well, for everything."

Personally, he thought she had it all wrong. He was the one who should be counting his lucky stars.

Chapter Seventeen

Audric looked at William and laughed. "Damn, man, you're snockered. You can't drink like you used to."

"You're a fine one to talk. Hell, you've fallen off that stool twice." William tried to appear indignant, but it was totally ineffective since he was weaving around like a seasick sailor.

"It wasn't my fault. Millicent's cleavage knocked me over. Gave me a clearer understanding of the American slang for breasts. Damn, that woman was blessed... and blessed... and blessed."

"I'm going to look foolish to my granddaughter if I don't brush up on her generation's... what do they call them? Something about bugs... damn, getting old sucks, I don't remember all the details like I used to." William rubbed his chin, frustration coloring his expression.

"Buzz words, but I don't think they say that anymore. You'll think you have it figured out, then it changes overnight, so don't bother." Audric gave the direction of the conversation a dismissive wave. "When's the last time you got your corn ground?"

"Hell, it's been so long, my cob qualifies as a born-again virgin. My mind is still firmly in the gutter, though—

that should count for something."

"I think getting a second shot at virginity requires your knob and mind to be playing from the same sheet of music." Audric downed the last of his ale before turning to his friend. "Time travel has one huge flaw in my humble opinion. If we're going back, I want to have my younger body. You know... for safety's sake."

"I'm calling horse hockey. You want to be able to wank the waitress, who is probably Charlotte's age, you dirty old geezer." Audric grinned because William was right. If he was younger... a lot younger, he would be leaving with the magnificent Miss Millicent for a few hours of sexual pleasure. "Not that I wouldn't enjoy a few rounds with my old libido. You know, now that I think about it, I can't remember the last time I... oh, hell, never mind. This conversation reminds me too much of my youth, and there weren't many parts of that I'd want to repeat."

Audric let out a deep sigh. He hated to admit it, but William was right. Being young and stupid had been exhausting and dangerous. As magicals with powerful skills and not much common sense, they'd made some terrible decisions. One of the worst had been the argument that cooled their friendship to the point, they hadn't seen or spoken to one another for almost a hundred years.

"Come on. I'm too tired to sit here pretending I want to be young again. That damned feather tick in your guest room will kill my back, but it's too late to travel tonight." Audric threw several gold coins on the bar, knowing he'd paid their tab and left their waitress enough extra she could probably take the next year off. The two men staggered to the door before nearly falling onto the sidewalk.

Ten minutes later, Audric looked around them in confusion. "I don't remember it taking this long to walk to your flat. Are you sure we didn't take a wrong turn somewhere?" Before William could answer, three thugs stepped out from the deep shadows of the alley.

Brandishing a knife, the tallest man stepped in front of the two wizards. "What have we here? Two old fools traipsing around the city after dark. Isn't it past your bedtime?"

"Probably. Thanks for your concern. I think we took a wrong turn." Audric saw William's hand slide into the deep pocket of his trench coat and knew he was going for his wand. He nor his friend needed a wand to do magic, but it added another layer of power to a spell and usually dazzled nonmagicals enough they backed off.

"That's it. Put your wrinkled old hand in your pocket and pull out your wallet. Grab your pocket watch, as well." Auric wanted to roll his eyes at the young fool's naivety. He and his friends were about to learn a very painful lesson. When the other two stepped up to him, Audric gave them a smile he knew didn't reach his eyes.

"You should follow your friend's example and reach slowly for your wallet. We watched you in the pub and know you're carrying gold coins. Hand them over, and you'll live another day." The second man wasn't Irish, but Audric couldn't immediately place his accent. The look on his face was sheer hatred, and Audric could feel anger pulsing around the man whose stare was as completely devoid of any hint of humanity. This man had sold his soul to the demons a long time ago, but it was the third man who sent a chill up Audric's spine. He stood back, his pose deceptively casual as he leaned against the brick wall. When he finally spoke, his voice reminded Audric of a snake, his tone more of a hiss than the over-confident style of his partners.

"Careful lads, I don't believe you know who you are dealing with."

"Tell us who you are, old man. I'll bet you're a rich old fool who carries his fortune in his pocket because you don't trust banks. Hand it over, and maybe we won't cut you up too bad. It would be a shame if your spoiled children couldn't identify your body."

Audric knew the second hoodlum had just signed his own death warrant, but he was content to stand by and let the other two paint themselves into the same corner.

"I'll give you nothing. Everything I own belongs to my granddaughter, and you'll not deny her a bloody red cent." William's shouted words bounced off the brick walls of the alley, making it seem as though he'd been standing in a mountain valley. His vehemence appeared to shock all three men, but it was the first dolt who made the mistake of moving first.

William pulled his wand from his pocket with a lightning-fast movement that was little more than a blur. With one stroke, the man standing in front of him fluttered to the ground, little more than a pile of ashes as his knife clattered to the ground at William's feet.

The second would-be robber ran into the shadows, but he never made it to the other end of the alley. Without enough time to turn the corner to put brick and mortar between him and the two wizards, the fool never had a chance. A bright fireball halfway down the dark path between two rows of businesses was the only indication he'd ever been on this earth. There wouldn't be anything left to clean up, so there was no reason to pull in backup.

Audric knew the third man was watching him for any sign of magic as the power the lower ranking wizard had been working so hard to conceal now shimmered around him in an aura only the Head of the Magic Council could see.

A split second of distraction was all it took. In the space of time no longer than it took Audric to glance at William, the third man pulled a wand from his pocket, the crackle of electricity making the hair on the back of his neck stand straight up. Before Audric could react, the other man screamed in pain, his wand suddenly red-hot burst into flames. The man was bound in a web so decorative it could have only been created by one person.

"I CAN'T LEAVE you alone for a minute." Brigitte stepped from the shadows, her wand still sparkling with residual energy. "Who is this asshat?" With a quick flick of her wrist, the man tilted to the side before tipping over and slamming unceremoniously into the damp cobblestone street. Gigi let him roll a few times before raising her finger. He was lifted in the air, dangling precariously while she turned back to her father.

"He's a dark wizard, Dad. If you two weren't snockered, you'd have noticed." She watched in utter disbelief as the two men leaned against each other and burst into uncontrollable laughter.

"Damn, I didn't see that one coming. I can't believe we had to be saved by your daughter. She's gorgeous, by the way—looks just like her beautiful mother." William's observation surprised her. Brigitte was rarely compared to her mother. Elizabeth Stafford had been stunningly beautiful, inside and out. Simply being considered in the same league as her mother was an honor.

"She does, indeed. Unfortunately, she inherited my mother's snarky disposition." Gigi shook her head at her father's ridiculous comment. He always said his mother was cantankerous, but his lovely wife disagreed. Elizabeth insisted her mother-in-law was a sweet woman who simply refused to put up with her son's arrogance. In Brigitte's opinion, it was probably a combination of the two.

"Lucky for you, I inherited *your* sixth sense and decided to check on you. After the message I received earlier, I was worried." He and William had been surrounded by magicals in the pub—some good and others not so much. Luckily, Millicent, was a friend who knew how to get word to Brigitte that her father and William were going to be easy marks when they left the tavern.

"How did you get here? Time travel wasn't in your skillset the last I knew."

Gigi shook her head in frustration. Damn, her pop was definitely toasted, and if William's swaying back and forth was any indication, he wasn't any better.

"It's not." *At least it's not a skill I've perfected.* "But there are Council members who are more than capable of sending someone through time. They will either pull me back in another four hours, or William can take us all back." Hopefully, the other man was sober enough to get them back to the present. She didn't care where they landed because she could handle the transport to the Council's hidden headquarters.

There wasn't any question the dark wizard bound and currently floating several feet above the ground was a low-level narc, who wasn't going to be able to give them any valuable information. The Council's interrogators wouldn't bother asking him questions. They'd just tap into his memory and pull out any information they could. They would make a token effort to rehabilitate him, but in the end, he'd be stripped of his magical powers, then his memory would be completely erased before being replaced with something so bland, it would bore the most conservative among them. *I hope they make him an incompetent accountant for a drug cartel.*

To his credit, the cretin whose buddies had tried to mug two wizards appeared to be marginally more intelligent than his pals, who were now little more than dust.

"There's no reason to whisk me off to your secret lair. I was paid two gold coins to stall you long enough for someone else to show up. They didn't tell me it would be a kinky witch with a rope fetish." Brigitte rolled her eyes at the man's admission. He'd just told the Head of the Council of Magic he'd sold them all out for less than the tip her father left the busty pub waitress.

"You're a special kind of stupid, aren't you? Do you even know who you're talking to?" William shook his head at the man, and with a quick flick of his wrist, a strip of duct tape appeared over the thug's lips. The man's eyes widened in surprise before narrowing in anger. "Yeah, that's going to hurt like hell when the interrogators pull it off. I'll bet you cry like a toddler, begging for mercy when they start probing around in that pea-sized brain of yours."

Brigitte bit the inside of her mouth, trying to suppress her laughter at William s taunting. She wasn't sure what business he was in, but it was obvious he was no one's fool. Audric stepped closer to the man and narrowed his eyes, his expression the same one she'd seen him use when dealing with a magical he found particularly offensive.

"Telling us you are useless is not in your best interest. Mr. Fitzpatrick has done you a huge favor. You should be grateful." Turning to William, he waved his hand in a circle, indicating he was ready to travel. "They ruined a perfectly good drunk. At least two of them got what they deserved. Take us back, and we'll introduce butt plug over there to the investigators at headquarters. You and I will get some rest, and my lovely daughter can make certain all the Adlers have gathered in Texas."

"What about Catalina and Cooper?" Gigi wasn't sure what it was about Catalina Adler, but she was worried about the other woman. They'd shared drinks and swapped stories of their lives a few weeks ago when Gigi was in Austin. Despite the obvious differences in their ages and abilities, Gigi had been surprised by the things they had in common—Cat's easy acceptance of the strange combination of Brigitte's position in the magical world and her struggles to fit in with the people around her. Learning Catalina often felt like an outsider in her own family surprised Brigitte and made the other woman seem more vulnerable than she first appeared.

"I've already sent them to Adler Oil. They are probably a bit disoriented by the abrupt move, but it was necessary.

The dark side tracking us through time changes everything. Let's go. I want to hand him over to the interrogators as soon as possible, and since a wild night with... oh, hell, never mind." William's laugh filled the night, and Gigi shuddered at the thought of knowing anything about her dad's thwarted sexual encounters.

Magicals were notoriously sexual, and from what she'd learned over the years, their sex drive didn't fade like their non-magical peers. Gigi and her sister speculated the *nons*, as they liked to call them, had much shorter lifetimes because they stopped having sexual intercourse as they aged. Spending time hidden in the back corner of the pub, watching her dad and William flirt with every woman in the place, Brigitte assumed they were going to be around for many years to come. Of course, that was contingent upon getting to the bottom of the dark side's subversive efforts to gain power.

Other members of the Council agreed with Brigitte— the threat was bigger than her dad wanted to admit. From the information she'd pulled together, there were too many accidental deaths associated with the pendants the five Adler mates and Bronx wore. She'd seen all the pieces and knew there was one for each point of the pentagram and hadn't understood why there were six until she'd seen Bronx and Kenya's pieces.

It hadn't been until last night, she'd finally sorted it all out. Finalizing the reconstruction of Lisa Star's journals provided the final clues she'd needed to solve the puzzle. Brighten Adler's plan to split the piece Lisa had stolen was brilliant. She'd known their children were fated mates, and the two halves of the final piece would have to be rejoined in order for the fulfillment of the powerful prophecy.

Brigitte's conversation with Catalina provided more evidence, and their brainstorming session proved how interaction and collaboration yielded more than what any of them could achieve individually. She looked forward to Catalina's mating—the increase in her magic was going to shock the woman who mistakenly believed her greatest skill was jewelry design. Gigi tried to explain how Cat's magic was vibrating just beneath the surface, but the other woman waved her off, unconvinced.

All of Gigi's prior research was confirmed when she met Catalina. It was the third Adler daughter who was the most like her mother and whose magic would eventually mirror Brighten's in strength and purpose. Her thoughts were interrupted when William sent the four of them hurtling through time. This trip was shorter, but the effect on their prisoner was devastating.

I am probably enjoying his misery more than I should, but when someone tries to kill my father, I feel entitled to a certain level of giddiness, watching the fool heave in the gutter.

Chapter Eighteen

B RONX STOOD AT the lake's edge, watching his family
confer with Audric, Brigitte, Charlotte, and Amaya.
The four of them were huddled a few feet from him,
talking quietly. Listening to them debate the best strategy
made him smile. Now, he understood why they hadn't
asked William to join them. It seemed the Stafford family
was a lot like the Adlers, preferring to hash out their
differences in private before bringing in an outsider to put
the finishing touches on a plan.

William stood to the side, deep in conversation with
Kenya. Watching his mate's expression for any indication
she was distressed by the way the conversation was playing
out, Bronx didn't see anything of concern. Deciding to
make certain she was coping, he connected with her
telepathically and was pleased when he heard the stream of
gratitude moving through her mind. He doubted she
would have been as receptive if William had simply shown
up and tried to insert himself into her life. It said a lot about
Kenya's connection with Audric that she'd recognized the
significance of his blessing.

"I'm looking forward to seeing how this goes down."

Bronx sighed as he turned around.

"Damn it, Cooper. I don't know how you manage to do it. Sneaking up on a shifter isn't easy—or smart." The man moved like smoke. Bronx had once compared him to a panther, and Catalina laughed. Shrugging her shoulders, she'd confided Cooper moved with even more stealth than Brooklyn. Bronx still found it difficult to believe anyone moved quieter than his younger sister. After years spent breaking into both homes and businesses to retrieve stolen goods for insurance companies, Brooklyn's skills had landed her on the most-wanted lists in more countries than Bronx could count.

When airports began implementing facial recognition software, Brooklyn relied on her best friend to hack into the systems, allowing her to continue traveling. Luke Grayson was now Brooklyn's husband, and Dom, his continued *adjustments* to the government's facial recognition database the only reason Brooklyn was able to leave their New Mexico home. Brooklyn and Catalina had lived close to each other when they were both based in New York. The two were still close, and Bronx smiled when he saw them standing nearby, their heads together, giggling like schoolgirls.

"Whoever yanked us home has some serious clout. I was ass-deep in a project for your Council of Magic when I saw Catalina walk into the bar where I was meeting a contact. Cam had been tracking her movement, and the last report he'd gotten had her in Europe. I still don't know how she managed to find me." Cooper shook his head, and Bronx had to hold back his laughter. Since he knew Audric was the one who'd summoned the two of them back to Texas, there was no question their exit would have been *abrupt.*

"It was like something out of a movie. There was a strange crackling sound all around us—like the world's worst case of static electricity. Hell, Catalina's hair started lifting, and the whole room started spinning. It was like being in a huge fucking washing machine filled with every imaginable color clothing, being washing in hot water. Everything was blurring together. When shit stopped moving, we were in her studio." Cooper shook his head again, this time, in a desperate attempt to get his bearings. Bronx suspected talking about the experience brought on a renewed sense of disorientation.

"Don't feel bad. I'm a time traveler, and it still kicks my ass. If you're prone to motion sickness, it's devastating."

"Is it the same process? Hell, I always wanted to travel by magic and move around in time, but I'm rethinking the whole thing." Bronx chuckled at Cooper's comment. Magic was like a lot of things in life—it looked a lot better from the outside. Cooper looked over his shoulder at the sound of a boat motor drawing closer. "Backup?"

"From what I've been told, this is the first time the Prairie Winds team and the Council have collaborated on such a large operation." Bronx knew Cooper would understand the significance. The more nonmagicals involved, the more likely their existence would be threatened by exposure.

"I understand your concern, Bronx, but I can assure you, Kent and Kyle only hire people they trust."

Giving the other man a nod, Bronx wondered how they would ever be able to keep a lid on this. He'd been a businessman long enough to know even the most loyal employee can be enticed to 'talk out of school,' as his dad used to say.

"I'm thrilled there are so many people willing to step up. Protecting these women is the only thing that matters." Turning over his amulet to Brigitte hadn't been easy, but she and Audric's argument was solid. Being asked to safeguard something didn't necessarily mean you were the best one to hold it forever. Oddly enough, it had been the youngest of his siblings who'd convinced him placing the piece in Brigitte's hands was best.

"Big brother, you did exactly what Mom planned. You kept it safe and found your mate. We both know nothing with our mother was ever done *by chance*." Simple words from a woman who held a special piece of all their hearts. The oldest nine Adlers had already been living on their own when they lost their parents, the loss had been heartbreaking, but only Paris lost her *home*. She'd been in the process of moving to college when she suddenly had no home to return to. Paris had relied on her siblings to stay anchored in the emotional storm.

Israel leaned close to Paris, whispering in her ear. She turned to look at him from where she was standing on the other side of the yard. After a short conversation with her husband and mate, Paris started toward where Bronx and Cooper stood. The irony of his speed demon sister being married to a sheriff still amused Bronx. At six foot seven, Trinity Stone was intimidating by any measure, but his love for Paris was easy to see in his expression anytime they were in the same space.

"I hear you've been thinking about me, big brother." Just a few inches over five feet tall, with long blonde curls and sparkling blue eyes, Paris was beautiful inside and out. Her outside beauty was easy to see, but people who knew her well always commented on the effervescence that seemed to bubble from deep inside her. The little imp elbowed him in the ribs and grinned. "Go ahead. Tell Cooper I'm your favorite sister; he'll figure it out eventually, anyway."

"You are impossible and spoiled rotten. Cleveland can't hold a candle to your penchant for speeding, and it's true... you are my favorite." Wrapping his arms around her, Bronx easily lifted Paris off her feet to turn two full circles with her in his embrace, just as he'd been doing since she was old enough to squeal in delight. As soon as he set her back on her feet, Bronx knew he'd made a mistake.

Trinity must have known what was coming because he was already sprinting toward them by the time Bronx set his sister back on her feet. She weaved back and forth, turned a distinct pea green, and slapped her hand over her mouth. Trinity didn't break his stride, scooping up his wife and sprinting back to the house. They disappeared inside within seconds, and Bronx felt like an ass.

"Probably not the way she'd planned on sharing the news, but effective nonetheless." Cooper's chuckle brought Catalina to his side.

"Paris didn't want to tell anyone until after the ceremony, but Charlotte hugged her and spilled the beans. We all promised to keep her secret until Bronx decided to play spin the sister."

"Thanks, Cat, like I don't already feel bad enough. I've greeted her like that since she was just a baby. I'd never do anything to hurt her—you, however, are ice dancing your way right to the top of my shit list." He was pleased to see her eyes alight with mischief as she walked into his arms.

"I've missed you, Bronx. You are almost as bad at keeping in touch as I am. We're a pathetic pair." She gave him a hug so tight, he felt his breath catch. Damn, he needed to start working out if his petite sister's hugs made his ribs ache. "Now, tell me how this is going down, and why is Lilly West in a boat with a fucking bazooka?" Cooper moved so fast, Bronx wondered if Catalina had claimed him or if he knew her well enough to anticipate her profanity.

"Language, Princess." The swat he'd given her lifted Cat to her toes, and the glare she gave him earned her a second strike. "If you think I'll be lenient because you are surrounded by family, you've made a grave error in judgment." Bronx bit his lip to keep from laughing at the phony look of contrition on Cat's face. Cooper was the only man Catalina ever submitted to, and he earned every moment of it. "Lilly may appear to be a wild card, but I assure you the woman is a crack shot. In addition, anyone who knows her would tell you there wasn't a chance in hell she was going to be left out of an operation less than a mile from her house."

"Are Dean and Del with her?" It was probably a given, but Bronx wasn't going to make any assumptions when it came to Kenya's safety.

"Oh, yeah. They know their lovely wife all too well. She's trigger happy on a normal day, and with the overabundance of adrenaline floating around... well, let's just say, Del and Dean know Lilly better than she knows herself. I'm sure they hope to keep her from making an impetuous decision. Realistically? I'd say their odds aren't great, but time will tell." Cooper's grin was so wide, Bronx figured even the non-shifters among them would be able to see it in the moonlight.

CATALINA FELT SOME of the tension drain from her muscles as she let herself relax when Bronx walked away. She was relieved when he'd excused himself to speak with Kenya before the ceremony started. Cat wasn't sure why her family suddenly made her uncomfortable... maybe it was because she was feeling the pressure of being the only one of ten who hadn't been able to commit to the man everyone believed was her mate. Damn it all to dancing dots, why had she been flying all over Europe looking for Cooper if she wasn't ready to make their relationship official?

When she shook her head, Cooper pulled her back against his chest wrapping his arms around her anchoring her in place. "What are you thinking about, Princess?"

"Wondering what the people in the bar thought when we disappeared in a colorful swirl of light." She felt his chest vibrate, his low laughter sending a warm rush of air over the shell of her ear. They'd both been exhausted after the unconventional trip; falling into bed had won out of sex, but now that she'd had a good night's sleep, her priorities were shifting quickly in the other direction.

"Interesting. Your answer was awfully vanilla, considering the way your body is reacting to my touch." She was wearing a dress Cooper bought for her before he'd left on his latest mission. She'd found it along with flowers and a hand-written note when she'd returned to her suite after a long night spent holed up in the workroom at the back of her store.

Save the dress... it's special, and I'm looking forward to being with you the first time you wear it. Don't forget to miss me... Love, C

It didn't take her long to figure out what was special about the dress when he helped her slip it on this evening. The entire garment was held together with hidden snaps. She'd been looking at the cloth-covered closures when he'd brushed his lips over the sensitive skin at the base of her neck.

"They are covered to muffle the sound of them being opened and closed in public."

Another reason he'd made certain she wasn't wearing panties or a bra. She wasn't busty, so bras weren't something she cared much about but panties? That was a different story. The dress hit several inches above her knees, which meant the lightweight, flowing fabric was moving around a lot in the Texas breeze.

"I think you are remembering what I said about this dress and wondering when I'm going to show you why I bought a garment I knew would make you question my sanity."

"I don't think you are insane. Arrogant, yes. Dominant, that's a given. A good choice as a personal shopper? That one doesn't look promising... Hell, now that I think about it, Dom seems questionable, too. Lots of chatter and not much delivery." Catalina knew she'd just thrown down a gauntlet, but desperate times called for desperate measures.

She hadn't seen Cooper in weeks, and since no other man held any appeal, she was suffering from a lack of the physical and emotional release only a half dozen orgasms provided.

"Talk to me, Princess. Tell me what we're watching. I'll be able to gauge how you're feeling about everything, so I won't ask those questions." Oh yeah, she could just imagine how he was going to monitor her reactions. Before she could respond, she felt the first snap release and his calloused palm slide over the hypersensitive skin above her mound.

"What will I find when my fingers slide further south, Princess? Are those smooth folds of yours slick with need?" His hand caressed her without moving, and she fought the need to wiggle enough to encourage his exploration. "Don't think I didn't recognize the challenge you just issued, Cat. I think you've missed lying over my knee?"

Had she ever.

"You're supposed to be narrating the scene. Let's test your ability to compartmentalize, shall we?" Oh shit, she didn't stand a snowball's chance in hell of passing this test. His fingers parted the petals of her labia, exposing her clit to his touch, eliciting a wash of liquid arousal to coat his fingers. "Your body behaves perfectly when your mouth isn't involved. Why is that, Princess?"

Wasn't it just like a damned Dom to ask questions on one topic while they wanted you to narrate a totally unrelated scene? Deciding the narration was the safer route, she tried to focus on the scene in front of them.

Chapter Nineteen

KENYA STOOD STOCK-STILL, watching as the other women took their places around the circle. Audric was lending his magic, along with several other members of the Council. No one seemed certain how they were going to account for six pieces instead of five. Contrary to what her mother had insisted, the medallion she wore had not rejoined the one Bronx's mother gave him. Wiggling her toes in the cool grass, Kenya appreciated the feel of the earth beneath her feet. The direct contact helped her feel more grounded and spiritually connected to the process. Feeling the planet's life force pulsing beneath her soles always soothed her in the way nothing else could.

"You're all doing great. Let your focus remain centered on allowing the power of Mother Earth to move through you—it will amplify your magic, letting us reach our goal more quickly." Kenya heard Audric's unspoken addition—faster equals safer. The sooner the magic totem was restored and back in the council's safekeeping, the better it would be for everyone.

Suddenly assailed by nerves, Kenya realized she was picking up the energy of everyone around her. The operatives—some seen, but many hiding in the shadows—

were balanced precariously on edge, their adrenaline spiking as they continuously scanned what she'd learned was their sector. The connection she'd felt to the magnetic power of the earth was shattering under the weight of her worry. Panic making her chest tight, her shallow panting breaths had jet black dots dancing in the yellow-gold light of the fire at the center of the circle.

Where's Bronx? I can't find him. I need to know he's here and safe.

"I'm right behind you, *Cheŕ*. I won't leave you." His large hands settled on the top of her shoulders, melting the tension from the rigid muscles with little more than a touch. His brothers stepped closer to their mates, and Bronx felt the power surge around them. When Audric, Amaya, and Brigitte started chanting the spell to reverse the centuries-old separation, Bronx could have sworn time slowed.

Placed on flat stones surrounding the fire, the medallions started to vibrate and glow. The eerie shade of green made him shudder when they seemed to be emitting tendrils of smoke trailing up several feet. When the wisps of smoke started forming the faces of the original witches at the separation ceremony, Kenya noticed her grandfather moved quickly to stand in the space to her right, blocking her view of Gigi. She wondered about the sudden change, but the question was answered when she heard the distant crack of a rifle shot.

"We had intruders who refused to stand down. They've been… *contained*. Continue mission… repeat, continue. Let's get this done. We're starting to attract too much attention." Kyle West's commanding voice came over the ear-bud Bronx was wearing, but she heard the words as if they'd been spoken directly to her.

Thank the great Goddess, the witches and wizards kept on as if nothing was happening around them. Kenya made every effort to tune out the radio chatter, knowing she needed to keep her attention and magical energy focused on the ceremony. Her skin started to tingle beneath the surface. The sensation was odd but starting to feel more familiar. A vision of her wolf trying to break free flashed through her mind as things around her started spinning out of control.

BRONX WAS GETTING more frustrated by the minute. The damned dark magicals were relentless. He could feel their malevolent energy surrounding them. He suspected the witches and wizards were simply testing the team, biding their time until the totem was restored. It was the finished product they were after. It was damned hard to focus when he heard Lilly inform the team, she had two intruders coming out of the lake just a few yards from where they were standing.

Lightning struck each of the medallions, melting them instantly, the liquid flowing in a counterclockwise stream, pooling in front of Audric. With a small circle of his finger, the wizard shrouded the area immediately, surrounding him in a blanket of thick white smoke. Out of the corner of his eye, Bronx saw Cooper take Catalina to the ground, covering her with his own body. Instinct kicked in, and Bronx followed suit with Kenya. From the sounds surrounding them, his brothers—whether by blood or marriage—had done the same.

A fireball raced across the surface of the water a split second before a thunderous boom sounded, echoing over the lake. The explosion on the shore put every fireworks display Bronx had ever seen to shame. He heard Kyle West shouting at his mom to stand down as burnt pieces of clothing floated down around them. By the time they were given the all-clear, Audric, Amaya, and Gigi were gone... along with the totem. The dead silence surrounding them was chilling—fortunately, it didn't last long.

"Holy shit. You all know how to throw it down." Tobi's excited voice sounded from his patio, and Bronx couldn't hold back his laughter when Kyle's and Kent's combined curses came over his earpiece.

Getting to his feet, Bronx was shocked to find the grassy area between his home and the lake had already been restored to its previous pristine condition. The rocks were gone, and there was no evidence of the fire that was burning in the center of the circle just moments earlier.

Looking up the gentle slope toward his home, he laughed out loud when he saw party lights draped between poles swaying in the breeze. Looking closer, he shook his head when he realized there were several elaborately fixed buffet tables with what he would bet was a feast.

"Why are they all standing down there?" Gracie's voice wafted on the breeze, and Bronx heard her husbands' frustrated voices coming from behind him. His brothers, blood and those he was blessed to call family by choice, lifted their mates to their feet, brushing off their surprise and laughing when Lilly bounced up to them, excited as the schoolgirl Bronx imagined she'd been. Wrapping Denali in a crushing hug, Lilly stepped back and grinned.

"Did you see the fireball? Damn, that gun is fucking awesome." By this time, all four West men had joined them as the rest of the team emerged from the shadows.

"Language, Darlin'. You know how Del gets when you curse." Dean's chuckle was all it took to break the stunned silence of everyone standing around in shock. Walking up to the house, Bronx held Kenya against his side, relieved to feel her relief.

"We're going to stay long enough for the debriefing, then we're heading inside to pack." Bronx knew they were never going to get any privacy with the entire Adler family in town, and he was determined to enjoy some alone time with his new mate. Cleveland and Israel had already been in touch with the Lamonts in Colorado. Bronx and Kenya would have use of their mountain cabin for the next several weeks.

"Really? We're going to the mountains? I've only seen the Rockies from Interstate-70." She was almost bouncing on the balls of her bare feet, excitement coming off her in waves. He was anxious for her to see how they were traveling. Austin had come through for him just before the ceremony started, confirming the company's smaller jet was ready to whisk them away as soon as they arrived at the private airport on the other side of the lake.

The flight wasn't long enough for a round of wild monkey sex, but that wasn't going to keep him from reminding Kenya who she belonged to. Now to get through enough of this damned party to look respectable. Whose damned idea was this, anyway?

Mine! Your plans to escape were just a bit too neat and tidy. You need to step up your game, my friend. Gigi's taunting voice moved through his mind, making him laugh despite his best effort to be annoyed with the blasted witch. Her day would come—sooner or later, he'd get his chance to exact a bit of revenge for her meddling.

Smiling to himself, Bronx led Kenya into the group, enjoying the hugs and slaps on the back as everyone celebrated. The third time he looked at his watch, the damned thing evaporated as Audric's laughter boomed around him.

Go… enjoy. You've earned it!

Epilogue

One Week Later

KENYA PAUSED AT the edge of the river, her heart racing as she looked behind her, waiting for her mate to catch up. In the past, running seemed like a punishment, but now, it was her favorite way to move around the mountain. Shaking her white fur, she tilted her head, listening for his approach. By the time she heard a twig snap to her left, it was too late, he'd already pinned her to the ground. Damn, how had he managed to circle around so quickly? It was damned humbling to find out she'd been gloating about outrunning him only to discover he'd beaten her at her own game.

Mine!

She loved telepathic communication when they were in their wolf. The intimacy ramped up her desire and her back arched in anticipation of his possession.

Yes, yours. Always.

We have time before we need to leave.

Kenya knew what he wanted and was more than happy to comply. Feeling his cock prodding her ass, his teeth pressed against the sides of her thick fur-covered neck.

Bondage was proving to be her kink. They'd tried several variations, but having his bite was definitely her favorite.

He'd claimed her ass the first night they'd arrived. She'd felt her wolf surge to the surface as soon as they stepped from the truck the Lamonts left for them at the airport. Kenya started to panic when her clothes began falling to the ground in tatters, but Bronx spoke into her mind, assuring her everything was as it should be. The popping of her bones as they moved into new positions was intimidating at first, but now, she was able to shift on the run.

Cher, stay in the moment, or you're going to walk down the aisle with a paddled ass. Now that I think about it, I would love to show everyone how beautiful your cheeks look when they're bright red.

He thrust into her so hard, Kenya yelped before groaning as the sting morphed into thundering need. His possession, the sound of the water tumbling over the rocky riverbed, and the cool breeze blowing in her face were all it took to send her soaring into an orgasm so powerful, she was barely aware of his howl as his release sent heated spurts deep in her ass.

Last night, Kenya was introduced to dinner at the Lamonts. Their glass tabletop hid nothing, and the Doms took great pleasure in baring their subs pink bits to their fellow diners. Katarina had been fondled by her husbands to orgasm twice before dessert. Several other club members joined them, and Kenya's embarrassment at having her legs spread wide, displaying her newly waxed pussy to everyone's view, faded quickly since the other subs were equally exposed.

"Shift, *Chef*." The sound of Bronx's human voice startled her out of her post-orgasmic stupor. Shifting quickly, she snuggled against him as he carried her the short distance to the elaborate home the Lamonts referred to as a cabin.

An hour later, Kenya walked into the living room to find Bronx staring out the floor-to-ceiling windows lining the front of the entire home. She'd been surprised how quickly the sun set behind the mountains and wondered if the locals ever missed seeing it set over water or a wide-open prairie. Kenya felt the moment he sensed her presence, his sharply indrawn breath the only indication he'd looked up from whatever he'd been watching.

"Fuck me, you are stunning, mate." He took in her short white lace dress and smiled. She'd been concerned it was too skimpy until she'd seen the appreciation in his eyes. "Lift the skirt and show me. I want to see your bare pussy decorated with the pretty pearls." He'd set her on the edge of the bathroom counter after her shower and spread her legs so wide, she was sure he'd been able to see her most hidden secrets.

The small pearl clip he'd attached to her pussy lips pushed them back, leaving her clit unprotected, and the smallest brush of air made her shudder. Getting dressed had been torture, and the simple act of walking down the hall had made her so horny, she'd been forced to pause twice to avoid coming without permission. She had no idea how she was going to walk down the cobblestone walkway to the Lamonts' gazebo over the creek, where they'd be legally joined as husband and wife.

Pulling her dress up far enough, the warm air from the fireplace brushing against her clit was enough to make her knees tremble.

"That's perfect, mate."

She was startled to realize he'd moved across the room to stand in front of her. Lowering her dress, he wrapped a jacket around her shoulders and led her to the door.

"Come on. Let's go get married."

The End

Books by Avery Gale

The Adlers
Brooklyn
London
Austin
Paris
Cleveland
Asia
Kensington
Israel
Bronx

The ShadowDance Club
Katarina's Return – Book One
Jenna's Submission – Book Two
Rissa's Recovery – Book Three
Trace & Tori – Book Four
Reborn as Bree – Book Five
Red Clouds Dancing – Book Six
Perfect Picture – Book Seven

Club Isola
Capturing Callie – Book One
Healing Holly – Book Two
Claiming Abby – Book Three

Masters of the Prairie Winds Club
Out of the Storm
Saving Grace
Jen's Journey
Bound Treasure
Punishing for Pleasure
Accidental Trifecta

Missionary Position
Another Second Chance
Star-Crossed Miracles
Dusted Star
Lilly's Choice

The Wolf Pack Series
Mated – Book One
Fated Magic – Book Two
Tempted by Darkness – Book Three

The Knights of the Boardroom
Book One
Book Two
Book Three

The Morgan Brothers of Montana
Coral Hearts – Book One
Dancing with Deception – Book Two
Caged Songbird – Book Three
Game On – Book Four
Well Bred – Book Five

Mountain Mastery
Well Written
Savannah's Sentinel
Sheltering Reagan

The Christmas Painting
Taking Out the Mother of the Bride

I would love to hear from you!

Email:
avery.gale@ymail.com

Website:
www.averygale.com

Facebook:
facebook.com/avery.gale.3

Twitter:
@avery_gale